"A RARE AND REMARKABLE ACCOMPLISHMENT . . .
Rick Bass takes the human heart and places it in the wilderness, physical and emotional. The result stands tall in American fiction."

—*The Virginian-Pilot* and *The Ledger-Star*

"*Platte River* is the most arresting tale. A large, powerful, outwardly contained man named Harley careens through life 10 miles north of the Montana border, always a few steps behind the woman he loves . . . Bass's vision is singular, his images refreshing."

—*The Orlando Sentinel*

"Exhilarating . . . Bass takes readers into a world unlike that of other writers. . . . The flights of imagination, the simple yet lyrical prose, the heightened scale of landscape and characters are unique. Anything is possible in a Bass story."

—*The Houston Post*

"Compelling . . . Beautifully written . . . Bass has a unique voice. His prose is peerless, as is his imagery. He has been described as 'the best young writer to come along in many years.' *Platte River* affirms this statement."

—*Rocky Mountain News*

"The natural settings of each story, all dominated by a river, are skillfully interwoven and form much of the rich texture of the stories. . . . Bass writes like no one else, and touches feelings—sadness, loneliness, freedom, wildness—that no other writer touches so deeply."

—*Grand Rapids Press*

"The tales have an almost magical intensity, born of clear, supple prose animated by stark and startling imagery. . . . What makes this a compelling book are [Bass's] finely detailed, complex characters, simple men and women crafted with sympathy and understanding."

—*Publishers Weekly*

PLATTE RIVER

BOOKS BY RICK BASS

PLATTE RIVER

RICK BASS

Ballantine Books • New York

First published by Houghton Mifflin Company.
This edition reprinted by special arrangement with Houghton Mifflin Company.

ACKNOWLEDGMENTS
These novellas first appeared in the following publications, in somewhat different form: "Mahatma Joe" in *Mississippi Review*; "Field Events" in *The Quarterly*; and "Platte River" in *The Paris Review*. Grateful acknowledgment is made to those magazines and to their editors—Frederick Barthelme, Gordon Lish, and George Plimpton, James Linville, and Elizabeth Gaffney, respectively. Debts accrued on my part for the editing help I received from Camille Hykes and Larry Cooper are too large to be accurately measured. Gratitude is also expressed to the publisher of this book, Seymour Lawrence, to Russell Chatham for painting the cover, and to Melodie Wertelet for the book's design.

Library of Congress Catalog Card Number: 94-96738

ISBN: 0-345-39249-3

Cover design by Ruth Ross
Cover art by Russ Chatham

Manufactured in the United States of America
First Ballantine Books Edition: July 1995
10 9 8 7 6 5 4 3 2 1

For Mary Katherine, Amanda,
Stephanie, Mary, and Mollie

CONTENTS

MAHATMA JOE

How many memorable localities in a river walk! Here is the warm wood-side; next, the good fishing bay; and next, where the old settler was drowned when crossing on the ice a hundred years ago. It is all storied.

— THOREAU, *January 1860 journal*

In February, after the chinook blew through, thawing people's faces into smiles and making the women look happy again, and making the men look like men again, rather than pouting little boys — in February, the preacher for the Grass Valley, Mahatma Joe Krag, began a rampage not unlike those of other springs.

It had been a hard winter in northern Montana, so hard that ravens sometimes fell from the sky in midflight, their insides just snapping, it seemed, and like great ragged clumps of black cloth they'd fall into the woods, or into a pasture, landing a few weeks shy of spring.

The stave-ribbed horses — those that the coyotes and wolves had not gotten — would go over and pick the crows up with their teeth and begin eating them, chewing the shiny black feathers.

There was nothing else.

People were so short-tempered that even the saloon closed down. In past winters they'd gone in to gather, socialize, drink, and complain collectively, but now people got into fights, pistol-pulling duels out in the snow, duels which never killed anyone, not at thirty yards with the .22 pistols the saloon kept on the counter for that purpose. The snow was usually swirling and blowing, which further lessened the risk, though often one of the duelists would injure the other, hitting him in the thigh or the shoulder, and even once, in the case of One-Ball Boyd, in the groin.

It was a bad winter, even for Grass Valley. The valley was long and narrow, and ran northwest-southeast along an old mountain range, the Whiteflesh Mountains, the first inland range off the Pacific. Storms came hauling off of the Siberian Peninsula and crossed the Bering Strait, kicking up eighty- and hundred-foot waves; they crashed into Alaska and then Washington, worked their way over the northwest passes, too strong to be stopped, and hurried over three hundred miles of prairie in eastern Washington, building up speed.

The Grass Valley was the first thing they hit. The valley was shaped like a bottleneck, slightly curved in the middle, and the storms slammed into it and rounded the curve, accelerating.

But it worked the other way during chinooks. Winds from the south raced up the same funnel, blowing hot air through the valley even in winter, melting all the snow in a matter of days, and launching new hatches of insects, buds in the fruit trees, and the smiles of women. Once February came around, the chinook could happen at any time. It became a race between south winds and north winds to see what got to the bottleneck valley first. The temperature could change almost a hundred degrees in twenty-four hours, going from twenty below to sixty or seventy above.

The chinook would last only a week at most, but it

was a sign that there would be just one more month of hard freezes left. A long time ago, the town had had a celebration called Naked Days, where no one wore clothes at any time, not even when they went in for groceries, not even when they went into the saloon. People fed their horses naked, slept naked for the first time in six months, and checked their mailboxes naked. There was hardly anyone around, and everyone knew everyone else. It was hard to describe the sense of freedom chinooks brought, after the entrapment of winter.

It had been great fun, that one week each year, the week of warm washes of wind against the bare chest and across the back, warm winds passing between bare thighs. The women all shaved their legs for the first time since the fall and lay out in the melting patches of snow down by the thawing river and got suntans. The men sat at picnic tables in the meadow behind the mercantile, also down by the river, and drank beer, wore dark sunglasses, and told stories. And there were no more duels — but that had all gone on in the old days, before Mahatma Joe Krag came into the valley, down from Alaska, angry and ambitious at not having converted anyone up there to Christianity, not even an Indian, in over six weeks. And now he hadn't scored big in Grass Valley in over twenty years: not since the day he left Alaska. He'd run out of souls up there. Little did he know that those six weeks would be the beginning of a rest-of-his-life drought.

Mahatma Joe put an end to Naked Days almost single-handedly, and it took him only a short time to do it.

He was mortified, during his first chinook, when he went into town and saw naked men and women walking down the streets, naked children playing catch, and was greeted by a naked storekeeper when he went in for his groceries. He was horrified but challenged, and sometimes, at night, delighted: he had found a valley more wicked than any of the mining camps in Alaska, and it was in the continental United States.

Mahatma Joe began to write articles about Naked Days for various evangelical magazines, inviting his fellow preachers to come to the valley the following February, during the next chinook, and witness "an entire valley of naked unsaved savages, and right inside our own country!"

The response was significant. The evangelists would watch the weather fervently in January, sometimes arriving early, anticipating the chinook's passage, calling it correctly even before the weather forecasters did. The evangelists prayed to the sky for the chinook to arrive, so that their business could begin.

The tradition faded. With all the visiting strangers, people in the Grass Valley began to keep their clothes on — around town, anyway.

Mahatma Joe pressed on to other, lesser matters.

He wanted the town to have rules, ever more rules. He wanted to stop the winter fights. He wanted to have a town church, a town Bible study, and a town vegetable garden in the rich meadowland along the Grass River. In summer he wanted the fruits and vegetables all picked and canned and bottled and sent to distant, savage lands. Joe believed that vegetables could calm angry souls, that meat — flesh! — was a temptation of Satan's creation.

Moose grazed in the fertile river meadow during the summer, and ducks floated on the slow blue waters. Elk, with their antlers in velvet, slept in people's yards in the high heat of the afternoon, and tried to get into the hay barns at night. The animals were unafraid of people in the hot windy months, and they would roll in the river's shallows like dogs, trying to escape the biting flies. Small children would walk out and touch the elk's antlers and feed them sugar cubes during those warm spells when rules dissolved.

Men and women would gather back in the saloon shortly before dusk to watch the sunset and discuss the day, telling of what they had seen. Ospreys. Nuthatches. Western flickers. Varied grosbeaks. Pine siskins. They knew all the names, though often would argue about which bird it was that had the crossed bill for cracking seeds. They loved seeing the western canaries, which were a bright yellow but had no song, made no noise.

There was hemlock, too, along the river in places, hemlock that would kill a man in half an hour. It looked like watercress, which some people used in salads. Every now and then someone would mistake hemlock for watercress, and it'd be the end. Everyone knew there were dangers still left to living up in Grass Valley. There were mountain lions, wolverines, bears, and wolves; it was one of the only places like that left.

Besides wanting to turn the entire river meadow into a town farm, a working, thriving plantation for the export of sweetness, Mahatma Joe wanted to get rid of the hemlock.

He spent the silent white winters huddled in the little office behind his cabin, writing venomous letters to editors of the many sinful newspapers across the country, and writing and rewriting various tracts on religion, sex, and education. He drafted and redrafted proposed ordinances. Joe had always imagined the little valley, ringed by snow and glaciers even in summer, as a new place to build something, a new place to get it right. But he needed help. He was sixty-eight by the time he had his final vision.

•

Sometimes people would move into the valley: young couples who filled in the places of the old-timers who had not made it through the winter. Occasionally they were young singles, a man or a woman running from some piece of extraordinarily bad luck, or a whole life of such luck; or sometimes they were young men and women who had just looked at a map, had seen that there were no paved roads leading into the valley and no towns within forty miles. They had seen how close it was to Canada, and they had wondered if, finally, this might be a place to rest.

They brought guns, traps, saws, books. They always brought a dog, and sometimes two or three, especially the single ones, and always the single women: hardy young women from Illinois and California, Texas and Arkansas, who had seen the name Grass on a map in some city or town library, on a day late in the fall, with end-of-day September light fading and flickering through the windows, with the library closing in half an hour and nowhere to go, no boyfriends, and life over too soon — everything over too soon, and somehow, too, everything just beginning. These women showed up every year, two or three of them, and asked around, found out who had died — who had fallen through the ice, who had been thrown from a horse, who had just disappeared — and they moved in, learning the old ways of the valley, quickly and hungrily, and staying, changing, learning.

One such woman moved to the valley in the fall of

Joe's sixty-eighth year, his twentieth year in the valley. Her name was Leena. She had no money, and she came unaware, came in from the South, and put an ad on the bulletin board outside the mercantile asking for a place to stay in exchange for labor — clothes washing, gardening, fence building, horse feeding, whatever. There were no vacancies, no empty cabins when Leena came. She lived in a tent down in the field behind the mercantile for three weeks, frying bacon and washing her hair in the nearby river at night, babysitting children in their homes and running the cash register in the mercantile.

Across the road from the mercantile, at the Red Dog saloon, the patrons played a game called Shake-a-Day: you rolled five weighted dice at once, and if you had three of a kind, you won a free drink. If you rolled four of a kind, you got a free six-pack, and if all five were the same number, you won half of the pot, which was all of the quarters that had been paid in since the last pot was won. The pot usually built up to six or seven hundred dollars before someone finally won it.

Leena would walk into the bar with her dog Sam, buy one drink and sip it slowly, enjoying the talk and learning things about the valley: the names of birds, the names of plants. Everyone sat on a stool with their dog beside them, and watched the dogs.

Leena would finish her drink, find a quarter, pay for her roll of the dice — you could roll only once a day — and lose, always. She never won a drink to take with her across the street and down to the river — a free drink that she could sip by herself while sitting on a boulder over the river, where she could watch the spry bats racing across the top of the current snapping at bugs, and the big trout beginning to leap, and night coming in, her new life in this bowl of a valley. She never won.

She bathed in the river at night. The water was frigid, with blocks of ice bobbing downstream like dirty heads of lettuce, floating past her as she scrubbed her body hard with the washcloth, fighting for breath, the cold taking the air from her lungs and turning her numb. The stars above her when she was in the river, gasping, seemed brighter than when she was not in the river. She had left the most selfish man in the world back in California. Each day of being away from him was a day of happiness, of getting stronger — feelings she never thought she'd have again. Leena would take a deep breath, dunk her head under the water, disappear from the moonlight, like one of the great trout that rose and then splashed back down. She would rinse her hair, scrub under her arms, open her eyes under water, look up at the wavering bright moon, and imagine that she was going to live all her life under the cold river, looking up. The gravel beneath her feet felt good.

She would shake violently then, it was so cold, and burst from the water and run for shore with numb legs, numb arms, sometimes tripping and falling, unable to run properly, with nothing working right at all. But she was clean, cleaner than she had ever been. She'd rub herself dry with a rough towel and crawl into her sleeping bag shivering and pull the bag's drawstring tight around her. Sam slept at her feet. Leena fell asleep with her face and hands still tingling from the river, her feet still numb, but the warmth inside her beginning to glow once more, like something that could never again be chilled. She was poor and her luck was bad, but she was clean.

Sam had been with Leena through three men, three men in six years. Things had fallen apart, lost their glue, like toys submerged in water, parts drifting away, shy parts, plastic parts that were never meant to last. They always wanted her to be a certain way, never wanted her to be able to change her mind or change anything. Leena fell asleep tingling, sinking, warm and safe, Sam's breath steady in her ear, with all the stars above her moving, rotating, sliding from view and back down behind the tall mountains as the earth spun. She would never have another man, not ever. They were like fish, they were wet, and they were all the same. There was no connection, no beauty. They just bit at the hook and were pulled in, and then they did nothing but lay there, gasping, their eyes turning slowly blue. Leena tumbled through her dreams, unimperiled by her lack of luck. She had never been so happy. She had never lived in so clean a place. Sometimes she thought she could sleep forever. It was good to be in a wild place where men didn't try to rule you.

Despite the deep good sleeps, Leena was up each morning at seven, frying bacon as the sun, a late riser, was only beginning to show over the tops of the tall mountains. Leena had a Frisbee, and she would go to the meadow with Sam and play, first thing every morning, right after breakfast.

Sam was daring, acrobatic, even heroic, chasing the Frisbee wherever it went, even diving into the river after it. He would race at full speed, tumbling over the little bluff and down into the water, never looking down to notice where the land ended and the river began. Surfacing immediately, he'd watch the Frisbee as it hovered in the air, just beyond his struggles, always a little too far away.

Leena would cry out whenever he did make a great catch, or even a great effort. She would clap her hands and pretend that she was a football coach, as her father had been, back in California. "Sammy my boy, that's what I like to see. That's the way to do it, Sammy boy!" she'd shout, laughing and clapping, delighted at Sam's excitement, his reaction to the praise.

Her laughter carried all the way up and down the narrow valley, trapped in the thin air, living forever in the thin air. Anyone could hear her. There were no secrets there. Everyone knew who Sammy was by the end of the first week.

A hawk's summer cry, drifting down over the ragged jumble of mountains, spread into the foothills and the valley's green, flat river bottom, which was no wider in some places than a freeway. Blue water cut through its middle. At noon, back in the woods, the loggers shut off their saws, sat down and opened their lunchboxes. Five or six miles away, on a still day, you could hear their laughter down in the valley, sometimes even hear their voices from up in the mountains, as if angels were speaking.

The valley was a park, green and forever, in the summer.

·

Leena thought how she wanted a horse with which to explore the mountains. She wanted a parrot, too, to talk to her, to ride around on her shoulder. Her life was a river across which she would build a bridge.

There would be one side, and then the other. Ray, owner of the mercantile, had told her that he had an old hay barn farther down the valley, and that he might sell it to her when winter came, if she still had not found a place to stay. There were holes in the roof, it was caving in, and the barn was full of years-ago, dry, no-good hay, but it would be better than the tent, and Leena began to apply her savings toward that, picturing it. She imagined the snow coming down as she sat at a table next to a lantern, writing letters, perhaps a letter to her parents, with the parrot on her shoulder and the horse in its stall, eating hay. Sam would be asleep at her feet. She would get a cat, too, to catch the mice.

No more men. She saved her wages, twelve dollars a day, for the winter. It was understood that whatever she had saved, no matter how much or how little, would be the actual purchase price of the barn. Leena knew that Ray was counting how much he paid her, counting how much she spent. She knew that he was watching. That was how men were: watchers, rule makers. But it was all right. After she bought the barn, it would be hers. This valley would be different. This valley still had wild promise.

The barn she was saving for was also along the river, farther upstream where the valley narrowed and the snows fell deeper. Whenever she moved in, Leena knew she would have to walk down to the frozen river with an ax and chop ice to get to the water for the horse to drink, and to get water for cooking. She would have to tie a rope around her waist to keep from getting lost in the heavy snows, and with that same rope around her, she would slip down through the hole into the cold water to bathe quickly. And she would fish through a hole in the ice, farther out, over the center of the river: she would build a fire to stay warm, a fire whose light would attract the dull, cold fish, and through the small hole she would catch them all, as many as she wanted, all night, and she would dry them, smoke them, hang them from the rafters to cure in the cold dry air, and her cabin would smell good, like fresh fish and smoke.

Leena thought about this as spring settled in around

them, and she saved her money, knowing these things —
for once knowing how something was going to be, and
for once in control.

She kept bathing in the river at night, her skin dark
when there was no moon. When she rolled over on her
back and let the cold water carry her downstream, bits
of moss and trout minnows brushed against her legs.
Breasts, shoulders, everything became shiny, luminous,
when the moon was out. Drifting into a fast current, she
would look up at the stars, the moon, and remember
only then that she might have gone too far. Breaking out
of her trance, she would swim hard upstream, moving
like a fish back to where she had started from, and clean.

.

What Mahatma Joe thought about in the spring-
going-to-summer, sitting alone in his tiny office with its
woodstove, listening to the sounds of dripping water
and the great cakes of ice sliding off his roof, melting
and losing their winter grip, was how he was nearing the
end, and how he was soon going to be accountable not
for the things he had done, but for the things he had not
done.

Not enough. He had done a lot, but not enough. He
had failed to *change* things, really. He had sent some
canned goods, jams and jellies mostly, to Africa from his
own modest garden each year. He buried people in the
valley when they died, and said words over them. He
had put down the Naked Days rebellion almost twenty
years ago. But he'd wasted time, too, wasted perhaps a
whole life, on other things: on long slow walks through
the woods, especially in the fall when the light was gold
and strange. He'd wasted time on sinful daydreams.
Sometimes, moving through that particular fall light,

Mahatma Joe pretended that he had already died and was in an afterlife. The light was so still, so different, and the woods so silent, that some days he believed it, that heaven was here and now, and not in need of alteration or correction.

Sinful!

Winters were spent in the office studying, making notes for imaginary sermons or for services to his wife and servant, Lily. Over the years, she'd heard it all, knew the answers better than he did, and corrected him in lilting, broken Eskimo-English when he faltered, or when he lost his thoughts to his age, forgetting even what it was that he was supposed to be studying. Lily had been his housekeeper in Alaska, and gradually over the years he had just stopped paying her. He had performed the wedding ceremony himself, though he wasn't sure if his license for such things had been current at the time.

"I haven't done anything," he'd tell Lily when he came back to the house late each afternoon. Thousands of pages of sermons, stuffed all around his office. The house would be warm, warmer than it had been in his drafty office, and supper would be cooking, vegetables and meat warming on the woodstove. Mahatma Joe shot moose and deer when they invaded his garden; bears and elk, too, anything that came slinking around looking for the Lord's produce. He hung the animals in the garage for Lily to skin and butcher. There was always meat.

When Joe came in sad and complaining, Lily would think of what she could say to cheer him up. "God loves you" was her favorite. That was usually the best one, the one he could not argue with when he came in sulky and self-abusing. Mahatma Joe had been a hero among some of the Inuit up in Alaska. He'd converted them to Christianity left and right, packing the church every Sunday, curing people in both their minds and their bodies, chasing fever from their blisters and wounds, and fever from their twisted, ecstatic, free souls, unsaved souls that didn't know the Word from the caw of a raven or the howl of wolves. Joe would shout at the heavens, shaking his fists and looking at his flock with wild eyes that frightened them, and made them want to change. It was as if he had come upon them in the woods and saved them, had fired a shot and killed or wounded some dark beast back in the woods just behind them. The Inuit had treated him like a king, and Lily believed that she'd been lucky enough to go with him when he left: proud to be such a strong man's wife, though sometimes she missed the pay she'd had when she was just a housekeeper.

That six-week slow stretch, when Joe had become disgruntled, and thought he was being called elsewhere — should they have stayed? Lily wondered. Would it have been evil for him to stay in Alaska and just be a regular man, instead of a saint? She understood the drama and attraction of saving souls — changing and controlling the course of a life, or lives — but Lily wondered often what it would have been like if, after running out of souls, Joe had just stayed there and been a regular preacher, just living a regular life instead of moving on and looking for fresh souls, like new meat, like a hunter.

That had been a long time ago. Things had gotten so different once Joe and Lily were across the border, in the Grass Valley. Despite its wildness, its lack of electricity or phones or a single radio station, the people were frightened of nothing, they were wild like animals, and happy — and Lily felt lost. She was shocked at the way they laughed at her husband — laughed at

him openly — though she did as Mahatma Joe had in-
structed her, and prayed for them anyway.

"I have to *do* something," he told her more and more,
as the days, and then the seasons, went sliding past,
surely moving faster than they had ever moved for anyone else. Joe had been a middle-aged man when he and
Lily came to the valley, strong and with a whole new
place before him. But now it was no different than how
it had ever been. In all of his sixty-eight years he had
done nothing.

Joe never received thank-you notes from any of the
agencies to whom he sent the jars of tomatoes, the preserved squash, the strawberry jam. He used not to mind
it, but as he grew older, it only added to the panic.

Except for Lily, he did not exist. It could already *be*
the afterlife, and it was not that much different from the
first life, because nothing was happening: nothing major,
nothing dangerous, not that he was aware of.

Lily cooked for him. They read magazines together,
talked about the garden, reminisced about Alaska, and
then compared their lives with those found in the
Bible, how what they had done or thought about during
the day reminded them of something someone had done
in a parable. Then they would go to bed.

They would undress and get under the covers together, still wearing their socks. Another day would slide
past as night drew up over them, while outside, in a hard
cold that dropped birds from midair, the stars glittered
and flashed through the trees, and all through the valley
coyotes howled and screamed.

Mahatma Joe would listen to the coyotes and think
that he was a sinner for doing *nothing,* and would be
startled to realize that he was breathing hard, almost
panting.

"*Ssshh,*" Lily would tell him, pulling him closer, patting his back, his shoulders, and his head, lowering it to her breasts. "*Sssh,* it be all right, *ssshh,*" she said, believing it was the coyotes that were alarming him, coyotes racing across the frozen snow, laughing and yapping, howling, running. "*Sssh,* it be all right," she would keep saying, and finally, falling into sleep, he would believe her, and would be grateful for it, as if she had come upon him in the forest with a gun and had killed a dangerous thing stalking behind him, and saved his life.

And then, after Joe was asleep, down in her breasts and warm like a child, Lily would put a pillow beneath his head. She would get out of bed, go into the kitchen, dress warmly, and put on the ice skates they had hanging on the wall, which they kept for when children sometimes came by, wanting to skate on the little pond below their garden. Lily kept the ice swept and scraped in winter for just that purpose. It was always ready, and on the rare occasions when children did come to the door asking if they could skate, Mahatma Joe was delighted. He would hurry down to the frozen pond with them, sit on a snowbank with his Bible, and read to them as they skated around and around the tiny hard pond, the sound of steel cutting through frozen water, steel scraping and flashing. The children, ignoring the Scripture, would have their fun as Mahatma Joe read on, tears coming into his old eyes, so much pleasure it brought him to be reading to an audience, to be touching young lives, the most important ones, and the tears would fall from his cheeks, freezing, like small bits of glass.

Lily would now take the skates out below that field of stars, the crunch of frozen snow, with the coyotes singing and howling, their cries echoing all around the narrow valley as if going in circles, start to finish and back to start again. She'd walk down to the pond and put the skates on, and with her hands behind her back and her chin tucked down, she would skate the way she and Joe had seen men and women do at a park in Seattle, so many years ago. It was a small pond, but she would skate as fast as she could anyway, using only her legs, slicing them back and forth like strong scissors, with the cold air racing past her face, and two moons to give her light: the real one cold as stone in the sky above her, and then the one frozen in the ice, reflected, the one that was just ahead of her and then beneath her, passing under her skates as she raced across it, an illusion, behind her, gone.

Lily would skate for hours, her long black hair flowing from beneath her cap. Her eyes watered with pleasure at the speed, and at the feel of it, and at the chance to be doing something that meant absolutely nothing at all, something other than gardening or cooking or cleaning — and she would skate until her legs were trembling, until she could no longer even stand.

She would lie down on the ice and rest, spread-eagled in the center of the pond. She would watch the moon, panting, her face bright as bone, and would imagine that it was watching her.

There were things to think about as she rested. It would be close to daylight now, colder than ever. The coyotes would be silent, resting too. There would be no sound at all. Lily would think about the other life, the one she had left.

Lily would remember Alaska, remember her friends, remember certain colors, certain days, like scraps of cloth. She would close her eyes, still spread-eagled on the ice, and think about her life with Mahatma Joe, and try to feel all of the water beneath her, an entire pond of water beneath the ice.

Sometimes she thought that she could feel it, that she

could sense there was something beneath all that ice. But she would grow quickly cold, lying still like that, and would have to get up and go back to the house, where she would hang the skates back up, build the fire again, slip out of her clothes and into bed with Mahatma Joe, who slept so soundly and who looked, each night (especially in winter), as if he were never going to wake up again. His brow would be furrowed, and Lily would smooth it with her thumb, and say again, "*Sssh, ssshhh, it be all right.*"

.

The chinooks came, and people behaved fairly well. Mahatma Joe walked down the roads looking for violators, but he rarely saw anyone, clothed or unclothed; the town had changed, especially in the last five years. There was talk of properly paving the road, which was studded with gravel and blue flecks of galena. The town was aging; growing softer, less wild.

The soil began to warm. The snow blanket shrank, spotted itself away, new ovals of earth and dry grass appearing larger each day, opening so suddenly that it surprised people, even though they saw it happen every year.

But it was never the same. Each year was a surprise. Each year winter fooled them, and they forgot all over again that earth and grass lay beneath the snow, that the world was not made of snow and ice, that the real world would reappear quickly when the grace of the chinooks arrived.

Mahatma Joe prowled the river bottom, explored the fecundity of the valley along the river near where Leena had her tent. He jabbed his walking cane into the rich mire. The cane made a sucking sound as he pulled it out.

Joe wanted the soil badly. He took handfuls of it home in his coat pockets and sprinkled it over his own poor garden. It occurred to him, and not for the first time, that these were his last days, but somehow he felt more free than he had in the past, felt cleaner, stronger.

It was like walking through the mountains for days and days — for years, even, without seeing anything — and then coming over a pass and looking out and seeing a small town below, glittering in the distance.

He knew, suddenly, that he was almost there, that he did not have far to go. He no longer had to conserve himself. His steps quickened.

Joe became extraordinarily protective of his home garden. Before, he had let the Arctic hares — their white pelage falling away, shedding to mottled summer brown — sit and warm themselves in the March light of his garden for a few minutes each day, nibbling on carrot tops like hungry sinners, before he sent Lily out to chase them away. Black bears, thin from the winter, sometimes moved in, digging in the garden for roots, and Joe would shoot them, and the elk and deer too, for the meat, but he knew this time that he would not need the meat, and he felt uneasy for the first time about killing, about taking lives too soon, too early.

Instead, Joe ran the moose and bears out of his garden with his chain saw. He kept it on the porch, and would crank it up and run out with it, revving it wildly whenever he saw anything near his vegetables, even the timid rabbits. Joe shot one black bear, a yearling, and hung it on a pole in the garden like a scarecrow, put a baseball cap on it and let it stand in the sun. Like a dark warm shadow, the black fur glistened at first but then fell away, as the winds carried most of the smell farther down the valley and up the river. Ravens flew in from the woods and rested on the bear's shoulders, leaning forward and picking at his fur as if leaning in to tell him a secret.

·

In April, Mahatma Joe's soil was no longer good enough for him. He had already managed to raise some beans and a few hardy tomatoes by covering them with blankets at night and by building small warming fires up and down the garden. And by midsummer, as ever, he'd probably be able to eke out enough produce to make his modest shipments to Africa again; but by the end of April, Joe was discouraged. What had been good enough for him in the past was no longer adequate, not since his visions of the larger, better gardens along the river. Joe cut the bear down from his pole, tilled up his garden in a rage, and burned the remains. There would be other good gardens in that very spot, but they would not be his, he knew.

Joe and Lily ordered more seeds from the catalogue and waited for the full moon. They bought another pair of skates at the thrift store for Mahatma Joe. Lily took him to the pond at night, under a moonless sky with stars glittering above like a throw-net cast over them, and on the thinning shield of ice she taught him to skate, for no other reason than that it was something he had never done before. She also taught him her tribe's songs, which he had once known but had long forgotten.

A full moon appeared. Joe and Lily prepared as if they were going to war, strapping shovels and spades across their backs like rifles, and though the center of the river had thawed and was running fast and cold down the middle, the shorelines were still frozen and packed hard.

They laced up their skates, stepped out on the ice, and pushed off, began to glide.

The racing water beside them drowned out the sound of their blades. Lily skated ahead of Joe, being younger and faster, and she leaped small logs that had fallen into the river and were frozen in the ice, leaping like the skaters they had seen in Seattle. Joe tried hard to keep up with her, to stay close to her, and he felt young, felt as quick as the dark river. He watched the moon on her back. He could not wait to get to the valley and sink the first bite of hoe into the centuries-old soil. He wanted to sprinkle the seeds on the dark upturned earth and let the moon's light touch them with its magic before he covered them up. He wanted to sing the songs of a sinner, in order to do good work. To do anything — any kind of work. To keep from disappearing.

·

She watched them from her tent. Sam's whines had awakened her the first night they came. Leena had thought they were bears until she heard their voices, almost like children's voices, over the strong night rush of the river.

Leena peered at their dark shapes moving along the river, the man and the woman discussing something, then separating, and beginning to swing scythes. The valley bottom was washed in moonlight, a light so bright it seemed brighter than daylight, though the slopes of the mountains and the trees were still in shadow, darker than ever.

But out by the river, in the tall spring grass, everything was silver, and she watched, a little frightened, as they moved through the grass with their scythes, cutting great sweeps of it down.

Renewed with every swing, Joe felt as if he were getting back at something, or as if he were earning something — felling sinners for the Lord, each blade of grass a dirty heathen. He was greedy with the scythe, and went at the grass as if it were an enemy or a threat. He delighted in the smooth ease with which it fell. Perhaps he was even saving souls.

Lily was enthusiastic as well. Forty-five years she had lived, and she'd never been in the midst of such tall, green, *growing* grass. She'd never used a scythe, never walked through waist-high grass, and the smell it made as it was ripped by the scythe almost brought water to her eyes. Her sweeps were smooth, wide, and rhythmic. Lily wanted to take her clothes off and lie down with old Joe in the deep grass under all that light, but knew they were on a mission, that there was only a certain amount of time left, and so she only thought about it, as she cut the grass, and it made her swings easier, gave them a better motion, until after a while she could almost believe that that was what she was doing, lying under the moon in the sea of grass with old Joe, rolling across the pasture in sweeping motions, and it made Lily's swings come easier still. She hummed to herself as she mowed the grass down.

Leena was frightened to see them in what she had come to think of as her field, and was frightened by the speed and force with which the moon-washed grass was disappearing. The man and the woman were working their way up the slope from the river, coming toward her tent, so that it almost looked as if they were searching for her, hunting for her in the tall grass — that that was the reason they were cutting it all down, bushwhacking it. But she had Sam with her, for protection, and she wanted to get closer, wanted to hear what they were saying to each other, and wanted to hear more closely the tune the woman was humming.

Leena thought that she might even want to help: it looked like it would feel good to cut that grass.

As she watched them, she was suddenly reminded of all the things she had been trying not to think about — California, and the last man, or the one before that. She had wanted to think only of herself. But in watching the grass fall, she was reminded of something else.

Leena crept out of the tent, one hand on Sam's collar, and began to crawl down through the grass toward the voices. She stopped when she had gotten close enough to make out their words and she lay flat, whispering to Sam to lie down beside her.

There was the sound of the river and of a breeze moving through the trees and the grass. The woman was sometimes humming, sometimes singing, using words that Leena had never heard before — such a song as might be used to put a child to sleep, or to keep a child from waking up; it was the kind of song that would mix in with the child's dreams, get tangled up in them. It made Leena want to sleep.

The man was calling out the names of vegetables as he worked. He was swinging hard, swinging the way Leena knew she would swing, though she admired more the grace of the woman's swings.

"Beans! Tomatoes! Kumquats!" snapped the old man, swinging as if his life were riding on it. "Beans! Tomatoes! Kumquats!" He kept repeating his chant as he moved up the hill, until he'd mown down an area sufficient to plant the crops he'd listed. Then he moved over and started a new section, imagining, Leena thought, what lay before him only a little ways into the future. He called out the crops with a strange sort of doubt, as if trying to force them into existence through sheer bravado.

"Corn! Okra! Taters!" he sang, swinging hard with the big scythe, but Leena could tell that he was getting winded, and that his fury, or fear, was doing him no good.

"Corn! Okra! Taters!" he wheezed in a hoarse voice as he drew closer. Leena had to lie down as flat as she could, clutching Sam to her side. They lay there as the scythe ripped the grass all around them, passing right over their heads, so close that she could have reached out and untied the old man's shoelaces. And then he was moving farther up the hill. He was silent now, but the sound of softly falling grass, like feathers, was all around them, and Leena shivered, delighted with her luck at not being discovered. She lay there like that until daylight, when Mahatma Joe and Lily stopped working and put their skates over their shoulders and walked out to the road toward home.

Leena watched them go and then stood up to shake the grass from her robe and out of her hair. It was a cold morning. The sun was not yet up over the mountains. No one in town was stirring. Leena walked down to the river, pulled her robe and boots off, left them on a rock, then dived into the center of the current, ripping the cold water with her body.

She floated down the river on her back, as she always did, reveling in the sting of the cold water, the way it assured her she was still alive, very alive, even if no one knew it. She thought about how what Mahatma Joe and Lily were doing seemed right, seemed good in a way that she could not define.

When the sun's crescent showed over the treetops, a gold corona promising the day to come, Leena pulled out of the current, turned over on her stomach, and swam back upstream to the rock, got out and dressed, her blood chilled to the center, but feeling strong, and she walked up the hill to her tent.

Fresh grass cuttings gathered on her boots and around her ankles as she walked. The morning smelled good. She wondered if men in this valley were different. She wondered if the women were different. She knew that everything else was — the weather, the seasons, the land. Perhaps other things were different as well.

·

The mercantile had a tall, steep roof, with old high windows through which dusty sunlight spilled, thin and dry, sunlight tasting of summer, even though it was only April and the river had still not completely broken up. Some days Leena might sell only an apple, or a tank of gas. There was a bell over the door that tinkled when it opened, but most days were silent. The loggers who lived throughout the valley couldn't get into the woods because of the frost breakup and the muddy roads; it would be another month before the logging trucks moved in and out of the valley, and with them the stumpy, bearded men with their heavy boots, their dirty hands, the orange suspenders holding up thick wool pants. The men wore hard metal hats. They left flecks of sawdust everywhere they went, so that Leena would have to sweep up after them whenever they came into the store to buy a candy bar, a piece of cheese and crackers, a soda pop.

Leena sat on the bench on the porch and worked at making a crude scythe out of scrap metal she had found, lashing it with wire to a sturdy green branch she'd broken off a tree. After her shift was up, she'd go into the woods looking for antlers. She wanted deer and elk antlers to use as a rake and pitchfork, and moose antlers to use as a shovel. Mahatma Joe and Lily had been coming every night, skating down the river along the rim of ice that grew smaller every day. They were planting now in the rich black river-bottom earth.

Some nights, as the moon grew darker, Leena would approach the edge of where they were working and sit, not afraid if they saw her or not, and half hoping they would, so that perhaps they would invite her to help. She had found some good elk antlers, and had made a strong rake.

But Joe and Lily never saw her in the tall night-waving grass. Mahatma Joe would walk down the furrowed rows, dropping the seeds in, still chanting each time a scatter of seeds fell — "Pumpkin! Pumpkin! Pumpkin!" — until Leena felt nearly crazy with the sameness of all of it. Lily would crawl behind Joe on her hands and knees, smoothing and patting the soil down tightly over the seeds in a careful, promising way that made Leena want to get to know Lily and be her friend.

Leena was delighted at the control that Lily and Joe had over the field: how they had cleared and planted it, and were now going to bring it to life and nurture it, controlling when things happened, when things were harvested. It seemed wonderful and simple, and she sat back in the darkness with her tools and waited to be asked to join them.

.

They were there every night, despite the waning moon. They napped during the day and let their house chores go to pot — dust accumulating, and weeds growing up around the cabin. Mahatma Joe had all but abandoned his Bible studies. He had been annoyed anyway at how he kept forgetting parts of it, parts he used to know well. They would wake up around four in the afternoon, when the shadows were beginning to grow longer, and with the light growing softer, shorter. They would open a can of soup or a tin of potted meat and eat it cold. They'd each drink a can of beer, because they felt it helped them skate better. The lane of ice running alongside the river was getting narrower each day, and they weren't sure what they were going to do when it all melted. There was only a thin strip left in places. Even in the shade of deep fir forests, bends in the river that never saw sunlight, there were young ovals of dark water beginning to appear in the middle of the ice sheet, dark patches of water that they skated around, ovals that were growing larger every night. The nights were growing darker, too, as the moon waned, and Joe and Lily had begun skating with flashlights, scanning the ice ahead of them for those deep holes, but still skating fast, skating hard.

Mahatma Joe didn't know what they'd do when all the ice was gone. He didn't own a horse. He did have an old birch-bark canoe, but he thought that would be too heavy to carry up the road each morning — four miles, and uphill. He considered Christ's uphill walk with the crucifix, and he wondered if maybe he could heft that canoe, if it was for a good cause — the garden — and was the last chance he had at, if not immortality, then at least salvation. Joe thought that he could, especially with Lily's help. Christ, after all, had had to carry his load all by himself; but he, Mahatma Joe, was luckier. Mahatma Joe had Lily to help him.

Joe would drink two beers, sometimes three, getting ready for the skating, and as the ice lane grew thinner and smaller, Joe began to believe more and more in the canoe.

After the third beer, Mahatma Joe didn't feel frail or old; he felt young, strong, the way he had felt twenty years ago, when he had first come into the valley looking for souls. He would let the current carry him and Lily down into Grass Valley where they would do their work in the garden, and then he would shoulder the canoe, balance it over his head and shoulders like a young man, a young man after souls, and start up the road. He had done it in Alaska, and he would do it farther south, in the Grass Valley. Grass Valley was no different. Joe was no different.

·

The garden grew. The bean plants were up first, ankle-high in the good soil. On their way down each night, Mahatma Joe and Lily now spent as much time jumping the black holes of river water as they did skating. They were in the air, it seemed, every fourth leg-stroke — skate, skate, skate, and then leap, up over a log or over a wide patch of water, and then skate, skate, skate, and then it was time to leap again. It was exhausting, but the beer, and the darkness of night, the black holes appearing right in front of them at the last second, made it exciting.

As the garden grew, Joe and Lily could not wait to get to it, and skated toward it eagerly each night, as if toward their children, to see what changes each day had brought. They felt light-headed, invincible, and it was not from the beers but from the thought of the garden, the strength of its growth, and the sureness that it was only going to get larger and larger.

"Beets! Carrots! Spinach!" Mahatma Joe would sing, preparing for each jump, calling out a vegetable for each stroke of the skates. He was becoming quite good at it, and was less afraid to jump than Lily, who was heavier than he was and who sometimes made the ice splinter when she landed.

It didn't seem right, Lily thought, that she should be carrying so many of the tools when she was heavier than Joe to begin with. It made Lily nervous, so she did not sing anymore, but concentrated, scanning with her flashlight as she tried to skate around the black holes when she could. But sometimes there was no choice, it was too late, and Lily had to leap. She would bite her lips and pretend she was like the people they'd seen in Seattle so long ago, the ones dressed up in glitter and sequins, skating under bright, swirling spotlights, leaping with abandon every time they got the chance. Everyone had applauded, including Joe and Lily.

It had reminded Lily of a dance they had done in her village when she was young, back before the old people had stopped dancing. She didn't remember much about it, didn't know why they did it, knew only that like all the dances, it was done to change something — either to force something to go away, or to force another thing into existence.

All the men in the village would put on feather costumes, wearing any kind of feathers they could; and all the women would form a circle around them and beat drums while the men hopped and danced and pretended to fly around.

It had been a long time ago. Lily knew that the men and women had worn beautiful ceremonial dresses, soft caribou hide, and necklaces made of caribou teeth that rattled when they danced. But she had been gone so long that her memory was beginning to erode. She was taking on an imaginary memory, one such as Joe might remember, where none of the women wore anything, and the men wore only their feathers and loincloths. In Lily's new, confused memory, that was how it was — the dancers had been stripped of all protection, all security, even all humanity, and were returning to the wild and to freedom. Lily remembered that it had been some sort of fertility rite, but whether for crops, or people, or fertility in general, she couldn't remember.

The dance had been held in a great wide pasture in the spring, she remembered, because the snow was leaving, and the nights were warm. She remembered being in the circle of women, watching the strange half-man, half-bird dance, the firelight flickering over them. She remembered being excited at the sound of the drumbeats and chants carrying off into the night, as if trying to change something, or perhaps trying to preserve something. She had never told Joe about it, because she knew he would disapprove of the dancing; and it was not something her village did anymore, anyway.

Lily thought about the children she'd never had. She thought about the life she had never lived, back in her old village. She thought about how it would have been different — neither better nor worse, but different — had she stayed. For a long time it had been enough just to share Joe's vision, just to be near it, but now Lily sometimes woke in the night convinced that she could not breathe. She believed what Joe told her about the next life, but there had been so little in this one that she felt almost ashamed of herself. Skating hard, Lily imagined that she could hear drumbeats that echoed her thinking. She imagined that she was wearing feathers; believed that Joe was *chasing* her, not just following her. For the first time in her life she wanted to get away from him, and she began to skate harder.

Lily turned her flashlight off to confuse him, and began skating all-out, as hard as she could. The river flowed north, into the Fishhead; Lily imagined that the Fishhead might still be frozen too, and that she could skate upriver on it, up through Canada and back into Alaska. She felt as if Joe had taken something of hers, had hidden it, and that she had no power, no manner of getting it back.

Lily could hear Joe's faint, surprised cries behind her. The slush and snow and sheet of floating ice cracked and splintered as she leaned forward and dug in, her dark eyes growing quickly accustomed to the night. She could hear the terror in old Joe's voice, the terror of being abandoned that all men and women knew. Smiling suddenly, Lily knew what the dance back in her village had been about: the men wanted to leave, but the women did not want them to. Those who could fly would be allowed to leave. But Lily did not remember seeing any of them take flight. She thought how Joe would look at the dance, how he would think it was mostly pathetic little half hops and jumps. She laughed, then, at what Joe would surely think was a silly backwoods idea, that any of them could control anything, whether it was the weather, or a crop, or even each other.

Almost surely, such a thought was nonsense.

Mahatma Joe was skating hard, gaining on her, and he heard her laughter, but that was all. If there had been a splash, it had not been distinguishable from the sounds of the river as it hurtled past, carrying cakes and rafts of melting ice along with it, tiny icebergs, pieces of winter, the last to change.

Joe coasted to a stop, turned his flashlight off, and sat down on the ice and cried. He cried as he stretched himself out over the ice. He cried with guilt. He felt the ice crack beneath him, felt the water racing just beneath it, water running in the wrong direction, to the north, against the flow of nature.

After he was through crying — and it did not take that long — he crawled carefully to the shore and took his skates off, hiked out to the road, and walked the rest of the way to the garden, listening to sounds in the night: birds, and the wind.

He walked hurriedly, hoping, in a sort of delirium of sadness, that he might find her in the garden when he got there, a kind of a miracle, her hoeing, having started without him. Had her laughter really been so quickly cut off?

Joe stopped on the rise above town and looked at his dark garden, at the still cabins that were spaced along the river, each with smoke rising from its chimney, and at the river itself, running through the little valley. Even from the ridge he could hear the sound of the rapids.

Joe watched the river, the light brighter over the valley than it had been back in the woods, and when he saw the pale, naked body come floating through the rapids, clearly alive, swimming upstream, and climbing out on the rock by the garden, Joe grew so excited that he fainted. But he was soon up and running across the field, arms outstretched, tripping but not quite falling, saved by love.

Joe ran down the hill with such speed that he imagined he could lift off and fly if he wanted to, though he did not make the attempt. Just knowing that he could, if he wanted to, was enough.

.

Sam rushed out barking, hackles raised, when Joe drew near the river. Leena, who was standing on the rock drying herself, did not know who it was at first, but then saw the skates hanging over his shoulder, and recognized the shape of his shoulders, his old head. Leena told Sam to stop barking, then asked the man where the other one was, the one who sang while she worked.

"She is gone," said Mahatma Joe. "I thought you were her. She is gone, and she took all her tools with her."

.

They worked until daylight, shoveling with the moose antlers, weeding with the hoe Leena had made out of the jaw of a moose. The elk antlers scratched good, deep furrows in the earth, like fingernails down her lover's back, Leena remembered, and then she remembered the way Lily had moved through the tall grass with the scythe, sweeping smoothly, sweeping hard, and Leena tried to do the same with her furrowing, her weeding.

The garden was knee-high in places. Joe had not asked her to put her shorts and shirt back on, and Leena had not wanted to; there seemed no need. The plants rubbed against her as she walked through them.

Once the sun's first rim of blaze came over the tallest line of mountains, she went to the river and bathed, and then got out and dressed.

They walked home quickly, Sam running in front of them. Leena carried her tent and clothes in her back-pack. They left the antler tools hidden in the garden.

"We will bring a bucket next time," Joe said. "We need to water the plants."

"I don't know how to skate," said Leena.

"That's okay," said Mahatma Joe.

.

Leena sat in the bow, and Sam in the middle. Mahatma Joe sat in the stern, watching them, and leaned back and trailed his hands in the cold ice-melt river. They had a lantern mounted on the bow, and as they pitched and slid over the little waves, curling up and over, sometimes splashing through the little haystack standing waves, the spray drenched Leena, blew back on Sam, and some of it even misted against old Joe; and the canoe's crazy slides and bounces pitched the lantern's light all over the woods, illuminating one side of the river and then the other, but it rarely showed them what lay directly ahead. Sometimes they would bounce into rocks, hitting them square on, throwing Joe and Leena out of their seats and making Leena drop her paddle. The boat would spin around, sliding down the little tongue of rapids backwards, and without a paddle, Leena would panic and begin to shout, clutching the sides of the boat, trying to will it to turn back around and point in the right direction — but they never capsized, they stayed low in the boat, and eventually they slid through the rapids, through the pitching waves and cool spray, and finally came back out into calmer water.

They would catch up with the paddle Leena had dropped; sometimes she would dive overboard and swim out to get it, in the still waters, and Sam, not wanting to be left alone in the boat with Mahatma Joe, would join her.

The ice along the shoreline was only the thinnest, most intricate paper crust; it was like lace, and Leena wondered how they could have stayed up on it. The nights were getting ever warmer, but the river was still as cold as it had been in winter. Leena had never felt water so cold, and swimming in it excited her.

It took her breath away and tried to numb her muscles and pin her arms at her sides; it tried to make her legs stop kicking and sink, unable to respond to her wishes; but Leena would hold her breath and fight against the cold, would keep swimming. The colder it was, the better she liked it. It was more of a challenge. It was more like being alive.

She would climb back into the canoe when she had the paddle, sliding over the gunwales like some river creature shining in the moonlight. Her teeth would be chattering as she sat back up in the bow. Leena would wring water from her hair to dry in the thin mountain air, slip on her dress, and rub her toes with her hands while Joe took the paddle and navigated, using the flat blade of the paddle as a rudder, looking around the shivering Leena and up ahead, trying to judge where the rocks were, trying to see beyond the lantern's dim glow.

Mayflies followed them down the river; moths swarmed around the lantern. Great brown trout leapt from the water, passing through the air in front of them, gulping moths attracted to the lantern light. The fish followed the canoe downriver, making Sam bark and lunge at them the whole way, almost upsetting the boat.

.

The moon had come back, and was full again. Leena would climb out of the canoe first, and then pull it farther up on shore so that Mahatma Joe could get out. Then she would begin carrying buckets of water up from the river. Each bucket held eight gallons; each full bucket weighed sixty-four pounds. Leena wore leather gloves but still developed red stinging blisters that made her want to cry, want to stop, but she knew that she couldn't, that Joe was not strong enough to carry the water, a big sloshing plastic bucket in each hand, and that if she did not do it, it would not get done.

Her arms felt strained, elongated even, as she hauled the full buckets up to the garden. By the time she got there, the cords in her neck felt stretched out as well. She had to walk pigeon-toed going up the small hill to get the power she needed, but the sound the soil made, drinking up the good water as she poured it, cold and loud, into the furrows, made the trips worth it, always worth it, no matter how much her neck and shoulders ached, no matter how red and tender the palms of her hands were becoming. Her hands would develop calluses soon enough, she knew.

Sam trotted along behind her on each trip to and from the river. The moon shone down on them. Elk and deer tried to approach during the night and nibble at the fresh growth. Mahatma Joe would move toward them through the waist-high beans like a predator, crouched down with one of the antler rakes. He would stalk the deer, then try to run up and attack them with the rake, though they always saw or smelled him coming, and with snorts and whistles they would bound away, white tails flagging, disappearing into the darkness. Joe would settle back down into the beans and wait for the next ambush as Leena emptied the river bucket by bucket, bringing what the garden needed, bringing the very water that perhaps had helped to drown Lily, that had filled, and then left, her lungs.

"Zucchini," Mahatma Joe would mutter to himself, crouched down in the garden. "Asparagus."

He thought of Africa, of dying dust babies, stomachs swollen from malnutrition, reaching their hands out for yams. He would get to heaven yet. He was doing a great thing.

Sometimes Joe would lie down on his side and nap, while all through the night Leena carried water, pouring it into the furrows, not ever having any idea what the garden was for, or why she was doing it — only that it was green and growing. She knew that it was responding to her touch, and she liked that. It made her feel a way that she had forgotten.

Leena vaguely realized that she was working for Joe, and that she was doing his work too, and for free, but she could not help it. She was amazed at the change. What once was meadow was now a cultivated garden, ordered and perfect. She'd quit working in the mercantile, had abandoned her hopes of buying the barn. There was room in Joe's cabin.

The soil splashed to mud as she poured the water; it splashed up around her ankles and got on her shorts, her shirt. Her hair was damp and scraggly from her exhaustion, and each time she went down to the river she wanted to set the buckets down and dive in, clean off, and float down the rapids. But each time, with the water so close, she could not resist making one more trip with the buckets instead, and one more after that, on into morning, until it was too late to swim, until the townspeople were up and moving around, starting the day. People had seen the garden, of course, but had no idea who the gardeners were; but now Joe and Leena were discovered. It did not matter; it was Joe's all-or-nothing garden, his gamble, and nothing mattered.

No one would bother his garden. He had created it, he had worked for it, and it was his. They would respect that.

·

Joe lay under the broad shade of a giant sunflower plant in the daytime and dozed. The days were dry and warm, the high mountain air thin. Leena would work on until midmorning, until she could carry no more water, and then, not caring whether anyone was looking, she would go over to her rock, strip, and dive in, feeling the dried mud and dust leave her body almost instantly as she plunged deep, her hair flowing around her, diving deep to the bottom, where there was moss and weeds that leaned downstream in the current and tickled her as she swam through it. At the bottom, she would grasp a handful of the weeds and hold on while the cold river pushed against her, cleaning her. She'd hold the air in her lungs and turn colder and colder until she could barely hold her breath any longer — the sun a bright glow above her, seeming closer than it ever seemed — and she'd release her grip then and swim for the top, up toward the brightness, and would break through the surface, gasping, the warm air a shock on her face, and she'd float on farther down with the current.

The men in the Red Dog saloon, loggers mostly, some of them having coffee, were still waiting for spring breakup. Some of them would be drinking beer already, at nine in the morning. They'd taken to sitting out on the porch to watch Leena, immensely grateful for her performance. Each time she went down, the loggers would make bets on how long she would stay under. She became a valley celebrity as she stood on the rock and toweled off, dry and clean again, and put her clothes back on. April turned into May.

She reminded the men of other times, long-ago times, of Naked Days, and of how their valley used to be clean, unchanged. The men who had been thirty-five and forty back then were almost sixty now, and everything had gone by, nothing would ever be the same, and yet nothing had happened.

There was nothing to do but wait for spring breakup, for the warm south winds to melt all the snow in the woods and to dry the roads. Then the men would go out into those woods and erase them, cut as many trees as they could, going back in time — they'd kill the old trees, and plant seedlings that would take ninety, a hundred, sometimes a hundred and fifty years to mature.

They watched Joe and Leena shoulder the birch-bark canoe and start up the road, carrying it like a crucifix. Once Joe and Leena had carried the canoe up around the bend in the road and were out of sight of the other men, Joe would set his end down, saying that his leg was hurting him, and Leena had to carry it herself the rest of the way.

Her back grew wide like a man's, and her arms grew large and tight. Leena would do what he told her to. She did not know why, only that she did.

They napped in the daytime in separate rooms: Leena on the couch, curled up with Sam, and Mahatma Joe in his room, clutching the pillow as if it were Lily. When dusk fell, they would take the canoe back to the river and begin their journey all over again. They liked working at night because it was not as hot, and they floated down the river toward their garden, dragging a net in the water behind them, lanterns mounted on both ends of the canoe. The net would be full of trout by the time they got there, and it was Leena's job to pull the heavy net up onto shore. Sam would bark and rush in, snapping at the net, alarmed by this writhing, gill-flapping pile. Joe had Leena carry the fish in buckets up to the garden — and he made her bury them alive, for fertilizer.

Leena moved as if in a trance. Her shoulders were now larger than a man's; her legs were thick and sturdy from carrying the canoe up the road every day. Her neck had nearly doubled in size. The night was hers. She no longer felt the need to bathe, and with her added muscle, found it harder to stay afloat anyway. The plants in the garden were chest-high, bearing fruit, and greedily, old Joe went from bush to bush, picking okra, lima beans, snap beans, and tomatoes, filling the plastic buckets with them and taking them to the canoe for Leena to carry home, where he would put them in jars and send them to other countries, remnants of his land, another country, different, but changing — souvenirs from a valley of men.

The loggers went back into the woods in late May. The last of the ice that had trapped Lily melted in June. Passing over that spot one night in the canoe, Joe and Leena looked down and saw her, perfectly preserved in the frigid waters, lying on the bottom, looking the same as she ever had, looking up at them through twelve feet of water as if nothing had ever happened, as if no days had ever gone by.

FIELD EVENTS

But the young one, the man, as if he were
the son of a neck and a nun: taut and powerfully filled
with muscles and innocence.

— RILKE, "The Fifth Elegy"

It was summer, and the two brothers had been down on a gravel bar washing their car with river water and sponges when the big man came around the bend, swimming upstream, doing the butterfly stroke. He was pulling a canoe behind him, and it was loaded with darkened cast-iron statues. The brothers, John and Jerry, had hidden behind a rock and watched as the big man leapt free of the water with each sweep of his arms, arching into the air like a fish and then crashing back down into the rapids, lunging his way up the river, with the canoe following him.

The brothers thought they'd hidden before the big man had spotted them — how could he have known they were there? — but he altered his course slightly as he drew closer, until he was swimming straight for the big rock they were hiding behind. When it became apparent he was heading for them, they stepped out from behind the rock, a bit embarrassed at having hidden. It was the Sacandaga River, which ran past the brothers' town, Glens Falls, in northeastern New York.

The brothers were strength men themselves, discus throwers and shot-putters, but even so, they were unprepared for the size of the man as he emerged from the water, dripping and completely naked save for the rope around his waist, which the canoe was tied to.

Jerry, the younger — eighteen that summer — said, "Lose your briefs in the rapids?"

The big man smiled, looked down, and quivered like a dog, shaking the water free one leg at a time, one arm at a time. The brothers had seen big men in the gym before, but they'd never seen anyone like this.

With the canoe still tied around his waist, and the rope still tight as the current tried to sweep the iron-laden canoe downstream, the big man crouched and with a stick drew a map in the sand of where he lived in Vermont, about fifteen miles upstream. The rapids surged against the stationary canoe, crashed water over the bow as it bobbed in place, and the brothers saw the big man tensing against the pull of the river, saw him lean forward to keep from being drawn back in. Scratching in the sand with that stick. Two miles over the state line. An old farmhouse.

Then the man stood, said goodbye, and waded back into the shallows, holding the rope taut in his hands to keep from being dragged in. When he was in up to his knees he dived, angled out toward the center, and once more began breast-stroking up the river, turning his head every now and again to look back at the brothers with cold, curious eyes, like those of a raven, or a fish.

The brothers tried to follow, running along the rocky, brushy shore, calling for the big man to stop, but he continued slowly upriver, swimming hard against the crashing, funneled tongue of rapids, lifting up and over them and back down among them, lifting like a giant bat or manta ray. He swam up through a narrow canyon and left them behind.

At home in bed that night, each brother looked up at the ceiling in his room and tried to sleep. Each could feel his heart thrashing around in his chest. The brothers knew that the big man was up to something, something massive.

The wild beating in the brothers' hearts would not stop. They got up and met, as if by plan, in the kitchen for a beer, a sandwich. They ate almost constantly, always trying to build more muscle. Sometimes they acted like twins, thought the same thing at the same time. It was a warm night, past midnight, and when they had finished their snack, they got the tape measure and checked to see if their arms had gotten larger. And because the measurements were unchanged, they each fixed another sandwich, ate them, measured again. No change.

"It's funny how it works," said John. "How it takes such a long time."

"No shit, Sherlock," said Jerry. He slapped his flat belly and yawned.

Neither of them had mentioned the big man in the rapids. All day they'd held it like a secret, cautious of what might happen if they discussed it. Feeling that they might chase him away, that they might make it be as if he had never happened.

They went outside and stood in the middle of the street under a streetlamp and looked around like watchdogs, trying to understand why their hearts were racing.

So young! So young!

They drove an old blue Volkswagen beetle. When the excitement of the night and of their strength and youth was too much, they would pick up the automobile from either end like porters, or pallbearers, and try to carry it around the block, for exercise, without having to stop and set it down and rest. But that night, the brothers' hearts were running too fast just to walk the car. They lay down beneath the trees in the cool grass in their back yard and listened to the wind that blew from the mountains on the other side of the river. Sometimes the brothers would go wake their sisters, Lory and Lindsay, and bring them outside into the night. The four of them would sit under the largest tree and tell stories or plan things.

Their father was named Heck, and their mother, Louella. Heck was the principal of the local school. Lory was thirty-four, a teacher, and beautiful: she was tiny, black-haired, with a quick, high laugh not unlike the outburst of a loon. Despite her smallness, her breasts were overly large, to the point that they were the first thing people noticed about her, and continued noticing about her. She tried always to keep moving when around new people, tried with her loon's laugh and her high-energy, almost manic actress's gestures to shift the focus back to *her*, not her breasts, but it was hard, and tiring. She had long, sweeping eyelashes, but not much of a chin. The reason Lory still lived at home was that she loved her family and simply could not leave. Lindsay was sixteen, but already half a foot taller than Lory. She was red-headed, freckled, had wide shoulders, and played field hockey; the brothers called her Lindsay the Red.

Lory was not allowed to work at the school where her father was principal, so she taught in a little mountain town called Warrensburg, about thirty miles north. She hated the job. The children had no respect for her, no love; they drank and died in fiery crashes, or were abused by their parents, or got cancer — they had no luck. Lory's last name, her family's name, was Iron, and one night the boys at her school had scratched with knives onto every desktop the words "I fucked Miss Iron." Sometimes the boys touched her from behind when she was walking in the crowded halls.

The night the brothers' hearts beat so wildly, they lay in the grass for a while and then went and got their sisters. Lory was barely able to come out of her sleep but followed the brothers anyway, holding Jerry's hand as if sleepwalking. She sat down with her back against the largest tree and dozed in and out, still exhausted from the school year. Lindsay, though, was wide awake, and sat cross-legged, leaning forward, listening.

"We went down to the river today," John said, plucking at stems of grass, putting them in his mouth and chewing on them for their sweetness, like a cow grazing. Jerry was doing hurdler's stretches, had one leg extended in front of him. There was no moon, only stars through the trees.

"Summer," mumbled Lory in her half sleep. Often she talked in her sleep and had nightmares.

"Who was your first lover?" Jerry asked her, grinning, speaking in a low voice, trying to trick her.

Lindsay covered her sister's ears and whispered, "Lory, no! Wake up! Don't say it!"

The brothers were overprotective of Lory, even though she was the oldest and hadn't had any boyfriends for a long time.

"Michael," Lory mumbled uncomfortably. "No, no, Arthur. No, wait, Richard, William? No — Mack, no, Jerome, Atticus, no, that Caster boy — no, wait . . ."

Slowly Lory opened her eyes, smiling at Jerry. "Got you," she said.

Jerry shrugged, embarrassed. "I just want to protect you."

Lory looked at him with sleepy, narrowed eyes. "Right."

They were silent for a moment, then John said, "We saw this big man today. He was pulling a boat. He was really pulling it." John wanted to say more, but didn't dare. He reached down and plucked a blade of night grass. They sat there in the moon shadows, a family, wide awake while the rest of the town slept.

·

They waited a week, almost as if they had tired or depleted the big man, and as if they were now letting him gather back his whole self. John and Jerry went to the rapids every day to check on the map in the sand, and when it had finally begun to blur, almost to the point of disappearing, they realized they had to go find him soon, or risk never seeing him again.

Lindsay drove, though she did not yet have her license, and John sat in the front with her and told her the directions, navigating from memory. (To have transcribed the map onto paper, even onto a napkin, would also somehow have run the risk of depleting or diminishing the big man, if he was still out there.) Jerry sat in the back seat, wearing sunglasses like a movie star and sipping a high-protein milk shake. John's strength in the discus was his simple brute power, while Jerry's strength — he was five years younger and sixty pounds lighter — was his speed.

"*Right!*" Jerry cried every time John gave Lindsay the correct instructions. In his mind, Jerry could see the map as clear as anything, and when John gave Lindsay a bad piece of advice — a left turn, say, instead of a right —

Jerry would shout out "*Wrong! — Braaapp! Sham-bam-a-LOOM!*"

There were so many turns to the road: up and over hills, across small green valleys, around a lake and down sun-dappled lanes, as if passing through tunnels — from shade to sun, shade to sun, with wooden bridges clattering beneath them, until Lindsay was sure they were lost. But Jerry, in the back seat, kept smiling, his face content behind the dark glasses, and John was confident, too. The closer they got to the big man, the more they could tell he was out there.

The road had crossed over the border into Vermont, and turned to gravel. It followed a small creek for a stretch, and the brothers wondered if this creek flowed into the Sacandaga, if the big man had swum all the way upstream before turning into this side creek, to make his way home. It looked like the creek he had drawn on his map in the sand.

Blackbirds flew up out of the marsh reeds along either side of them. They could feel him getting closer. There was very much the sense that they were hunting him, that they had to somehow capture him.

Then they saw him in a pasture. A large two-story stone house stood at the end of the pasture, like a castle, with the creek passing by out front, the creek shaded by elm and maple trees, and giant elms that had somehow, in this one small area, avoided or been immune to the century's blight. The pasture was deep with rich green summer hay, and they saw a few cows, Holsteins, grazing there.

Again, the man wasn't wearing anything, and he had one of the cows on his back. He was running through the tall grass with it, leaping sometimes, doing *jetés* and awkward but heartfelt pirouettes with the sagging cow draped across his wide shoulders. He had thick legs that jiggled as he ran, and he looked happy, as happy as they had ever seen anyone look. The rest of the cattle stood in front of the old house, grazing and watching without much interest.

"Jiminy," said Lindsay.

"Let's get him," said John, the strongest. "Let's wait until he goes to sleep and then tie him up and bring him home."

"We'll teach him to throw the discus," said Jerry.

"If he doesn't want to throw the discus, we'll let him go," said John. "We won't force him to."

"Right," said Jerry.

But force wasn't necessary. John and Jerry went into the field after him, warily, and he stopped spinning and shook hands with them. Lindsay stayed in the car, wanting to look away but unable to; she watched the man's face, watched the cow on his back. The cow had a placid but somehow engaged look on its face, as if it were just beginning to awaken to the realization that it was aloft.

The big man grinned and put the cow back on the ground. He told them that he had never thrown the discus, had never even seen it done, but would like to try, if that was what they wanted him to do. He left them and went into the stone house for a pair of jeans and tennis shoes and a white T-shirt. When he came back out, dressed, he looked even larger.

He was too big to fit into the car — he was as tall as John but thirty pounds heavier, and built of rock-slab muscle — so he rode standing on the back bumper, grinning, with the wind blowing his long, already thinning hair back behind him. The big man's face was young, his skin smooth and tanned.

"My name's A.C.!" he shouted to them as they puttered down the road. Lindsay leaned her head out the window and looked back at him, wanting to make sure he was all right. The little car's engine shuddered and shook beneath him, trying to manage the strain. The back bumper scraped the road.

"I'm Lindsay!" she shouted. "John's driving! Jerry's not!"

Her hair swirled around her, a nest of red. She knew what Lory would say. Her sister thought that all the muscle on her brothers was froufrou, adornment, and unnecessary. Lindsay hoped that Lory would change her mind.

"Lindsay, get back in the car!" John shouted, looking in the rear-view mirror. But she couldn't hear him. She was leaning farther out the window, reaching for A.C.'s wrist, and then higher, gripping his thick arm.

"She's mad," Jerry howled, disbelieving. "She's lost her mind."

A.C. grinned and held on to the car's roof, taking the bumps with his legs.

.

When they drove up to their house, Lory had awakened from her nap and was sitting on the picnic table in her shorts and a T-shirt, drinking from a bottle of red wine. She burst into laughter when she saw them approach with A.C. riding the back bumper as if he had hijacked them.

"Three peas in a pod," she cried. She danced down from the table and out to the driveway to meet him, to shake his hand.

It was as if there were three brothers.

From the kitchen window, Louella watched, horrified.

The huge young man in the front yard was not hers. He might think he was, and everyone else might too, but he wasn't. She stopped drying dishes and was alarmed at the size of him, standing there among her children, shaking hands, moving around in their midst. She had had one miscarriage, twenty years ago. This man could have been that child, could even have been that comeback soul.

Louella felt the blood draining from her face and thought she was dying. She fell to the kitchen floor in a faint, breaking the coffee cup she was drying.

It was the end of June. Fields and pastures all over the Hudson Valley were green. She had been worrying about Lory's sadness all through the fall and winter, on through the rains and melting snows of spring, and even now, into the ease of green summer.

Louella sat up groggily and adjusted her glasses. When she went outside to meet A.C., she could no longer say for sure whether she knew him or not; there was a moment's hesitancy.

She looked hard into his eyes, dried her hands on her apron, and reached out and shook his big hand. She was swayed by her children's happiness. There was a late-day breeze. A hummingbird dipped at the nectar feeder on the back porch. She let him come into their house.

"We're going to teach A.C. how to throw the discus," said Jerry.

"Thrilling," said Lory.

·

He had supper with the family, and they all played Monopoly that evening. Louella asked A.C. where he was from and what he did, but he would only smile and say that he was here to throw the discus. He wasn't rude, he simply wouldn't tell her where he was from. It was almost as if he did not know, or did not understand the question.

They played Monopoly until it was time for bed. The brothers took him for a walk through the neighborhood and on into town. They stopped to pick up people's cars occasionally, the three of them lifting together.

There was a statue of Nathan Hale in the town square, and, drunk on the new moon, drunk with his new friends, A.C. waded through the shrubbery, crouched below the statue, and gave the cold metal a bear hug. He began twisting back and forth, pulling the statue from the ground, groaning, squeezing and lifting with his back and legs, his face turning redder and redder, rocking until he finally worked it loose. He stood up with it, sweating, grinning, holding it against his chest as if it were a dance partner, or a dressmaker's dummy.

They walked home after that, taking turns carrying the statue on their backs, and snuck it into Lory's room and stood it in the corner by the door, so that it blocked her exit. It still smelled of fresh earth and crushed flowers. Lory was a sound sleeper, plunging into unconsciousness as an escape at every opportunity, and she never heard them.

Then A.C. went downstairs to the basement and rested, lying on a cot, looking up at the ceiling with his hands behind his head. John and Jerry stayed in the kitchen, drinking beer.

"Do you think it will happen?" Jerry asked.

John was looking out the window at the garden. "I hope so," he said. "I think it would be good for her." He finished his beer. "Maybe we shouldn't think about it, though. It might be wrong."

"Well," said Jerry, sitting down as if to think about it himself, "maybe so."

John was still looking out the window. "But who cares?" he said. He looked at Jerry.

"This guy's okay," said Jerry. "This one's good."

"But do you think he can throw the discus?"

"I don't know," Jerry said. "But I want you to go find some more statues for him. I liked that."

.

That first night at the Irons' house, A.C. thought about John and Jerry, about how excited he had been to see them walking up to him. He considered how they looked at each other sometimes when they were talking. They always seemed to agree.

Then he thought about John's hair, black and short, and about his heavy beard. And Jerry, he seemed so young with his green eyes. His hair was blond and curly. A.C. liked the way Jerry leaned forward slightly and narrowed his eyes, grinning, when he talked. Jerry seemed excited about almost anything, everything, and excited to be with his older brother, following him down the same path.

Later, A.C. got up from his cot — he'd been sleeping among punching bags and exercise bikes, with dumb-bells and barbells scattered about like toys — and went quietly up the stairs, past Lindsay's room, through the kitchen, and into the living room.

He sat down on the couch and looked out the big front window at the moon and clouds as if watching a play. He stayed there for a long time, occasionally dozing off for a few minutes. At around four in the morning he awoke to find Lory standing in front of him, blocking the moon. She was dark, with the moon behind her lighting only the edge of one side of her face. He could see her eyelashes on that one side. She was studying him almost the way Louella had.

"Look," he said, and pointed behind her.

The clouds were moving past the moon in fast-running streams, like tidal currents, eddying, it seemed, all to the same place, all hurrying by as if late to some event.

"What is that statue doing in my room?" Lory asked. She was whispering, and he thought her voice was beautiful. A.C. hoped he could be her friend too, as he'd become a friend of her brothers. He looked at the moon, a mottled disc.

"Do you want to sit down?" he asked. He patted the side of the couch next to him.

Slowly she did, and then, after a few seconds, she leaned into his shoulder and put her head against it. She put both her hands on his arm and held on.

After a while, A.C. lifted her into his lap, holding her in both arms as if she were a small child, and slowly he rocked her. She curled against him as tightly as she could, and he rocked her like that, watching her watch him, until dawn.

When it got light, she reached up and kissed him quickly, touching his face with her hands, and got out of his lap and hurried into the kitchen to fix coffee before anyone else was up. A few minutes later, Louella appeared in the living room, sleepy-eyed, shuffling, wearing a faded blue flannel robe and old slippers, holding the paper. She almost stepped on A.C.'s big feet. She stopped, surprised to see him up so early, and in her living room. He stood up and said, "Good morning," and she smiled in spite of herself.

Around eight o'clock John and Jerry got up, and they chased each other into the kitchen, playing some advanced form of tag. The lighter, faster Jerry stayed just ahead of John, leaping over the coffee table, spinning, tossing a footstool into his path for John to trip over. Lory shrieked, spilled some milk from the carton she was holding, and Louella shouted at them to stop it, tried to look stern, but was made young again by all the motion, and secretly loved it — and A.C., having come meekly in from the living room, stood back and smiled. Louella glanced over at him and saw him smiling, looking at the brothers, and she thought again of how eerie the fit was, of how he seemed to glide into all the right spots and stand in exactly the right places. It was as if he had been with them all along — or even stranger, it was as if he were some sort of weight or stone placed on a scale that better balanced them now.

After breakfast — a dozen eggs each, some cantaloupes, a pound of sausage split among them, a gallon of milk, and a couple of plates of pancakes — the brothers went out to their car and tossed all their throwing equipment in it — tape measure, discs, throwing shoes — and they leaned the driver's seat forward so that A.C. could get in the back, but still he wouldn't fit.

He rode standing on the bumper again. They drove to the school, to the high, windy field where they threw. From there it seemed they could see the whole Hudson Valley and the knife-cut through the trees where the river rushed, the Sacandaga melting through the mountains, and on the other side the green walls of the Adirondacks. A.C. looked around at the new town as they drove. He thought about Lory, about how soft and light she'd been in his arms, and of how he'd been frightened by her. Riding on the back of the tiny car reminded him of being in the river, swimming up through the rapids: all that rushing force, relentless, crashing down over and around him, speeding past. Things were going by so fast. He looked around and felt dizzy at the beauty of the town.

.

There was a ring in the center of the field, a flat, smooth, unpainted circle of cement, and that was where the brothers and A.C. set their things and began to dress. The brothers sat down like bears in a zoo and took their street shoes off. As they laced up their heavy leather throwing shoes, stretching and grasping their toes, they looked out at the wire fence running along the south end of the field, which was the point they tried to reach with their throws.

A.C. put his shoes on, too, the ones they had given him, and stood up. He felt how solid the earth was beneath him. His legs were dense and strong, and he kicked the ground a couple of times with the heavy shoes. A.C. imagined that he could feel the earth shudder when he kicked. He jumped up and down a couple of times, short little hops, just to feel the shudder again.

"I hope you like this," said Jerry, still stretching, twisting his body into further unrecognizable shapes and positions. He was loosening up, his movements fluid, and to A.C. it was exactly like watching the river.

A.C. sat down next to them and tried to do some of the stretches, but it didn't work for him yet. He watched them for half an hour, as the blue air over the mountains and valley waned, turning to a sweet haze, a slow sort of shimmer that told A.C. it was June. Jerry was the one he most liked to watch.

Jerry would crouch in the ring, twisted — wound up — with his eyes closed, his mouth open, and the disc hanging back, hanging low, his knees bent. When he began to spin, it was as if some magical force were being born, something that no other force on earth would be able to stop.

He stayed in the small circle, hopping from one foot to the other, crouched low, but with the hint of rising, and then he was suddenly at the other end of the small ring, out of room — if he went over the little wooden curb and into the grass, it would be a foul — and with no time or space left in which to spin, he shouted, brought his arm all the way around on the spin, his elbow locking straight out as he released the disc, and only then did the rest of his body react, starting with his head; it snapped back and then forward from the recoil, as if he'd first made the throw and then had a massive heart attack.

"Wow," said A.C., watching him unwind and recover and return, surprisingly, to a normal upright human being.

But John and Jerry were watching the disc. It was moving so fast. There was a heavy, cutting sound when it landed, far short of the fence, and it skidded a few feet after that and then stopped, as if it had never been moving.

.

Jerry threw two more times — they owned only three discs — and then the three of them, walking like gunslingers, like giants from another age, went out to get the discs. The brothers talked about the throws: what Jerry had done right, and what he had done wrong. His foot position had been a little off on the first throw. He hadn't kept his head back far enough going into the spin of the second throw. The third throw had been pretty good; on the bounce, it had carried to the chain-link fence.

John threw next, and then Jerry again, and then it was John's turn once again. A.C. thought he could do it himself. Certainly that whip-spin dance, skip, hurl, and shout was a thing that was in everyone. It had to be the same way he felt when he picked up a cow and spun through the tall grass, holding it on his shoulders. When it was his turn to throw the discus, he tried to remember that, and he stepped into the ring, huffing.

A.C.'s first throw slammed into the center of the head-high fence and shook it. John and Jerry looked at each other, trying not to feel amazed. It was what they had thought from the beginning, after all; it was as if he had always been with them.

But A.C.'s form was spastic. It was wrong, it was nothing. He threw with his arms and shoulders — not with his legs, and not with the twist of his wide back. If he could get the spin down, the dance, he would throw it 300 feet. He would be able to throw it the length of a football field. In the discus, even 230 feet was immortality.

Again, the brothers found themselves feeling that there was a danger of losing him — of having him disappear if they did or said the wrong thing, if they were not true and honest.

But the way he could throw a discus! It was as if their hearts had created him. He was all strength, no finesse. They were sure they could teach him the spin-dance. The amazing thing about a bad spin, as opposed to a good one, is how *ugly* it looks. A good spin excites the spectators, touches them all the way down and through, makes them wish they could do it — or even more, makes them feel as if they *had* done it, somehow. But a bad throw is like watching a devil monster changeling being born into the world; just one more awful thing in a world of too many, and even spectators who do not know much about the sport will turn their heads away, even before the throw is completed, when they see an awkward spin. A.C.'s was, John and Jerry had to admit, the ugliest of the ugly.

His next throw went over the fence. The one after that — before they realized what was happening, or realized it too late, as it was in the air, climbing, moving faster than any of their throws had ever gone — rose, gliding, and hit the base of the school. There was a *crack!* and the disc exploded into graphite shards. One second it was there, flying and heroic, and then it was nothing, just an echo.

"A hundred and ten bucks," Jerry said, but John cared nothing for the inconvenience it would bring them, being down to two discs, and he danced and whooped, spun around and threw imaginary discs, waved his arms and continued to jump up and down. He danced with Jerry, and then he grabbed A.C.

"If you can learn the steps . . ." John was saying, almost singing. The three men held one another's shoulders and danced and spun across the field like children playing snap-the-whip. John and Jerry had never seen a discus thrown that far in their lives, and A.C., though he had felt nothing special, was happy because his new friends were happy, and he hoped he could make them happy again.

Riding home on the back bumper, the air cooling his summer-damp hair and clothes, he leaned against the car and hugged it like a small child, and watched the town going past in reverse now, headed back to the Irons' house, and he hoped that maybe he could make them happy forever.

The brothers bragged about him when they got home, and everyone listened, and like John and Jerry they were half surprised, but they also felt that it confirmed something, and so that part of them was anything but surprised.

John was dating a schoolteacher named Patty. A shy-eyed Norwegian, she was as tall as he was, with freckles and a slow-spreading smile. A.C. grinned just watching her, and when she saw A.C., she would laugh for no real reason, just a happy laugh. Once when John and Jerry had gone to their rooms to nap, A.C. went outside with Lindsay and Patty to practice field hockey.

A.C. had never played any formal sports and was thrilled to be racing across the lawn, dodging the trees and the women, passing the ball along clumsily but quickly. Patty's laughs, Lindsay's red hair. If only he could live forever with this. He ran and ran, barefoot, back and forth in the large front yard, and they laughed all afternoon.

·

On the nights when A.C. did not stay with the family, he returned to the old stone house in Vermont. Some days he would swim all the way home, starting upstream at dusk and going on into the night — turning right where the little creek entered the Sacandaga, with fish bumping into his body and jumping around him as if a giant shark had passed through. But other nights he canoed home against the rapids, having loaded boulders into the bottom of the canoe to work his shoulders and arms harder. After he got home, he tied the canoe to the low branch of a willow, leaving it bobbing in the current.

Some nights in the farmhouse, A.C. would tie a rope around his waist and chest, attach the other end of it to one of the rafters, and climb up into the rafters and leap down, swinging like a pirate. He'd hang there, dangling in the darkness. He'd hold his arms and legs out as he spun around and around, and it would feel as if he were sinking, descending, and as if it would never stop.

He would tell no one where he had come from. And he would forget the woman in Colorado, the one he was supposed to have married. Everyone comes from somewhere. Everyone has made mistakes, has caused injuries, even havoc. The woman had killed herself after A.C. left her; she had hanged herself.

This is what it's like, he'd think. This is the difference between being alive and being dead. He'd hang from the rope and spin. This is the only difference, but it's so big.

Sometimes he would sleep all night dangling from the rafters: spinning, a bit frightened, hanging like a question mark, only to awaken each morning as the sun's first light filtered through the dusty east windows. The sound of the creek running past just out front, the creek that led into the river.

·

There were mornings when Lory was afraid to get up. She thought it was just common depression and that it would pass with time, but some days it seemed too much. She slept as much as she could, which seemed to make it worse and worse. She tried to keep it a secret from her family, but she suspected that her brothers knew, and her mother, too. It was like drowning, like going down in chains. And she felt guilty about the anguish it would cause others.

But her brothers! They anchored her and nourished her, they were like water passing through her gills. If they came down the hall and found her just sitting in the hallway, her head down between her knees, they — John or Jerry, or sometimes both of them — would gently pick her up and carry her outside to the yard, into the sun, and would rub her back and neck. Jerry would pretend to be a masseur with a foreign accent, would crack Lory's knuckles one by one, counting to ten some days in German, others in Spanish or French, mixing the languages to keep her guessing, to make her pay attention. Then he would start on her toes as John continued to knead her neck muscles and her small, strong shoulders.

"Uno, dos, *trey*," Jerry would hiss, wiggling her toes. He'd make up numbers. "Petrocci, zimbosi, bambolini, *crunk!*" he'd mutter, and then, "The little pig, he went to the market. He wanted beef — he wanted roast beef . . ."

He'd keep singing nonsense, keep teasing her until she smiled or laughed, until he had her attention, until he'd pulled her out of that well of sadness and numbness, and he'd shake his finger at her and say, "Pay attention!" She'd smile, back in her family's arms again, and be amazed that Jerry was only eighteen, but knew so much.

They would lie in the grass afterward and look up at the trees, at the way the light came down, and Lory would have the thought, whenever she was happy, that this was the way she really was, the way things could always be, and that that flat, vacant stretch of nothing-feeling was the aberration, not the norm; and she wanted it always to be like that, and still, even at thirty-four, believed that it could be.

When they were sure she was better, one of the brothers would walk to the nearest tree and wrap his arms around it, would grunt and lean hard against it, and then would begin to shake it until leaves began to fall. Lory would laugh and look up as they landed on her face and in her hair, and she would not pull them out of her hair, for they were a gift, and still John or Jerry would keep shaking the tree, as if trying to cover her with the green summer leaves, the explosion of life.

·

A.C. and the brothers trained every day. When A.C. stayed at the farmhouse, each morning shortly before daylight he would get in his canoe and float all the way to Glens Falls, not ever having to paddle — just ruddering. As if following veins or arteries, he took all the right turns with only a flex of his wrist, a slight change of the paddle's orientation in the water, and he passed beneath dappled maples, flaking sycamores, listening to the cries of river birds and the sounds of summer as he slipped into the town.

Besides hurling the discus outside near the school, the brothers lifted weights in the school's basement and went for long runs on the track. Each had his own goal, and each wanted A.C. to throw the unspeakable 300 feet. It would be a throw so far that the discus would vanish from sight.

No one believed it could be done. Only the brothers believed it. A.C. was not even sure he himself believed it. Sometimes he fell down when entering his spin, trying to emulate their grace, their precision-polished whip-and-spin and the clean release, like a birth, the discus flying wild and free into the world.

In the evenings the whole family would sit around in the den watching *M*A*S*H* or the movie of the week — *Conan the Barbarian* once — their father, Heck, sipping his gin and tonic, fresh-squeezed lime in with the ice, sitting in the big easy chair watching his huge sons sprawled on the rug, with their huge friend lying next to them. Lindsay would sit in the corner, watching only parts of the movie, spending more time watching Lory — and Lory, next to her mother on the couch, would sway a bit to her own internal rhythm, smiling, looking at the TV screen but occasionally at the brothers, and at A.C.

The nights that A.C. stayed over, Lory made sure that he had a pillow and fresh sheets. Making love to him was somehow unimaginable, and also the greatest thought of all; and he had this silly throw to make first, this long throw with the brothers.

Lovemaking was unthinkable — the waist-to-waist kind, anyway. If she gambled on it and lost, she would chase him away from the brothers as well as herself.

The idea was unthinkable. But each night she and A.C. would meet upstairs in the dark, or sit on the couch in the living room, dozing that way, with Lory in his arms, curled up in his lap, her head resting against his wide chest. That was not unimaginable.

A.C. trained all through the summer. Early in the evenings, sometimes the brothers went out looking for statues with him. Their back yard was becoming filled with statues, all of them upright just outside Lory's and Lindsay's windows. A.C. laid them down in the grass at daylight and covered them with tarps, but raised them again near sundown: long-ago generals, riverboat captains, composers, poets.

Louella kept her eye on him, suspecting, and believing in her heart, that he was the soul of her lost son come back in this huge body, come home finally. She did not want him to love Lory — it seemed that already he was too close — but she did not want him to go away, either. Louella watched A.C. carefully, when he could not see she was watching him. What would it have been like to have three sons? What would that third son have been like? She felt both the sweetness and the anguish of it. She could not look away.

•

He had not been so happy in a long time. He was still throwing clumsily, but the discus was going farther and farther: 250, 255 feet; and then 260.

Each was a world-record throw, but the brothers did not tell A.C. this. They told no one else, either. It was the brothers' plot to not show him off until he was consistently throwing the astonishing 300 feet. Perhaps A.C.'s first public throw of the discus would not only set a world's record; perhaps he'd hurl it so great a distance that no one would believe he was from this earth. Sportswriters and fans would clamor after him, chase him, want to take him away and lock him up and do tests on him, examine him. He would need an escape route, the brothers imagined, a way back to the Sacandaga River, never to be seen or heard from again . . .

The plan got fuzzy at that point. The brothers were not sure how it would go after that, and they had not yet consulted with A.C., but they were thinking that somehow Lory would figure in it.

Certainly they had told no one, not even their mother — especially not her.

A.C. was euphoric as the summer moved on. When he was back at his farmhouse, he often went out to the pasture and lifted a cow and danced around with it as if it were stuffed or inflated. Or in Glens Falls he'd roll the brothers' little Volkswagen gently over on its back, and then he would grab the bumper and begin running in circles with it, spinning it like a top in the deep grass. The muscles in his cheeks tensed and flexed as he spun, showing the most intricate striations. His veins would be visible just beneath his temples. A.C. would grin, and John and Jerry thought it great fun, too, and they'd get on either end and ride the upside-down car like a playground toy as A.C. continued to spin it.

The summer had not softened him; he was still all hard, still all marvelous. Children from the neighborhood would run up and touch him. They felt stronger, afterward.

Lately, on the nights he stayed over at the Irons' house, once everyone else was asleep, A.C. would carry Lory all through the house after she had fallen asleep in his lap. He imagined that he was protecting her. He carried her down all the hallways — past her parents' room, her brothers', past Lindsay's, into the kitchen and out to the garage: it was all safe and quiet. Next he took her into the back yard, among the statues, and then into the street, walking through the neighborhood with her as she slept.

There was a street called Sweet Road that had no houses, only vacant lots, and trees, and night smells. He would lay her down in the dew-wet grass along Sweet Road and touch her robe, an old fuzzy white thing, and the side of her face. The wind would stir her hair, wind coming up out of the valley, wind coming from across the river. He owed the brothers his happiness.

Some nights, far-off heat lightning flickered over the mountains, behind the steep ridges. She slept through it all in the cool grass. He wondered what she was dreaming.

.

Late in the afternoons, after practice, the brothers walked the mile and a half to the grocery store in town, and along the way they showed A.C. the proper discus steps. Lory and Lindsay followed sometimes, to watch. The brothers demonstrated to A.C., in half crouches and hops, the proper setup for a throw, the proper release, and he tried to learn: the snap forward with the throw, and then the little trail-away spin at the end, unwinding, everything finished.

Jerry brought chalk and drew dance steps on the sidewalk for the placement of A.C.'s feet so he could move down the sidewalk properly, practicing his throws. Like children playing hopscotch, ducking and twisting, shuffling forward and then pretending to finish the spin with great shouts at the imaginary release of each throw, they moved through the quiet neighborhood, jumping and shouting, throwing their arms at the sky. Dogs barked at them as they went past, and children ran away at first, though soon they learned to follow, once the brothers and the big man had passed, and they would imitate, in the awkward fashion of children, the brothers' and A.C.'s throws.

Lory could see the depression, the not quite old part of herself, back behind her — back in June, back in the spring, and behind in winter; back into the cold fall and the previous dry-leaved summer — but she was slipping forward now, away from all that. A.C. took her to his farmhouse and showed her how to hang from the ceiling. He'd rigged the harness so that she could hang suspended and spin.

He had to get over the fear of injuring someone again. Had to hit the fear head-on and shatter it. He had run a long way to get here. He was ready to hit it head-on. It was worth it, once again. And he wanted her to be brave, too.

"It feels better naked," he said the first time he showed

it to her, and so she took her clothes off. Lory closed her eyes and put her arms and legs out and spun in slow circles around and around, and A.C. turned the light off, sat down against the wall, and watched her silhouette against the window, watched her until she fell asleep, and then he took her out of the harness and got in bed with her, where she awoke.

"We won't tell anyone," he said. She was in his arms, warm, alive. It made him dizzy to consider what being alive meant.

"No," she said. "No one will ever find out."

She fell asleep with her lips on his chest. A.C. lay there looking at the harness hanging above them, and wondered why he wanted to keep it a secret, why it had to be a secret.

He knew that this was the best way to protect her, and that he loved her.

He stayed awake all through the night, conscious of how he dwarfed her, afraid that if he fell asleep he might turn over and crush her. He rose before daylight, woke her, and they got in the canoe and drifted back to New York State, and were home before dawn. A.C. crept into the basement that first night, and every night thereafter.

Lory had not liked hanging from the ceiling. She didn't know why, only that it had frightened her. She kept the harness with her, kept it hidden in her drawer. She just wanted to love him, was all.

.

Many evenings the family had grilled corn for dinner, dripping with butter. They sat outside at the picnic table and ate with their hands. Night scents would drift toward them. As darkness fell, they would move into the house and watch the lazy movies, the baseball games of summer, and then they would go to sleep. But Lory and A.C. stayed up later and later as the summer went on, and made love after everyone had gone to bed, and then they would go out on their walk, A.C. still carrying Lory, though now she remained awake.

When she was not too tired — when she did not need to go to bed — they would paddle the canoe upriver to his farmhouse, with Lory sitting behind A.C. and tracing her fingers on his wide back as he paddled. The waves would splash against the bow, wetting them both. They moved up the current slowly, past hilly, night-green pastures with the moon high above or just beyond their reach. Summer haying smells rose from the fields, and they passed wild tiger lilies growing along the shore as they crossed into Vermont. Lory felt weightless and free until it was time to go back.

They lay on the old mattress in the farmhouse, with holes in the roof above them, and through the roof, the stars. No brothers, thought Lory fiercely, clutching A.C. and rolling beneath him, over him, beneath him again; she knew it was like swimming through rapids, or maybe drowning in them. Her brothers protected her and understood her, but A.C. seemed to know what was in the center of her, a place she had believed for a long while to be soft and weak.

It was exciting to believe that perhaps it was strong in there. To begin to believe she did not need protecting. It made his protection of her all the more exciting, all the more delicious — unnecessary, and therefore extravagant, luxurious.

This new hardness and strength in her center.

They sat on the stone wall in front of the farmhouse afterward, some nights, before it was time to leave, and they watched the cattle graze under the moon, listening to the slow, strong, grinding sound of their teeth being worn away as their bodies took nourishment. Lory and A.C. held hands and sat shoulder to shoulder, cold and still naked, and when it was time to go, they carried their clothes in a bundle down to the stream, the dew wetting their ankles, their knees, so that they were like the cattle as they moved through the grass — and they'd paddle home naked, Lory sitting right behind A.C. for warmth against the night.

.

The brothers continued to train in the daytime, and as the summer ended, there was a haze over the valley below them. They were throwing far over the fence, better than they'd ever thrown in their lives. They were tanned from the long hours of practicing shirtless. The sisters came by with a picnic lunch while the men threw. They laid out an old yellow Amish quilt that had belonged to their mother's mother, with the hexagon patterns on it looking not unlike the throwing ring in which A.C. and the brothers whirled before each heave of the discus. The sisters would lie on the quilt on their stomachs, the sun warm on the backs of their legs. They ate Swiss cheese, strawberries, and apples, drank wine and watched the men throw forever, it seemed, until the sisters grew sleepy in the sun and rolled over and looked up at the big white cumulus clouds that did not seem to be going anywhere. They closed their eyes, felt the sun on their eyelids, and fell hard asleep, their mouths open, their bodies still listening to the faint tremors in the earth each time the discus landed.

A.C. had stopped sleeping altogether. There was simply too much to do.

He and Lory would go for canoe rides out on Lake

George, only they would not take paddles with them. Instead, A.C. had gotten the harness back from Lory, and he slipped that over himself and towed her out into the lake as if going to sea, bare to the waist, and Lory in her one-piece suit. They were both brown from the picnics, and with nothing but the great blue water before them, they appeared to glow red, as if smudged with earth. The sunlight seemed to focus on them alone, the only two moving, living figures before the expanse of all that water, out on top of all that water. Their bodies gathered that solitary light so that they were upright, ruddy planes of flesh, of muscle, dull red in that late summer light, and with nothing but blue water beyond.

A.C. waded out, pulling the canoe with Lory riding inside, sitting upright like a shy stranger, a girl met on the first day of school in September. And then thigh-deep, and then deeper, up to his chest, his neck — he would take her out into the night.

Once they were on the lake, he would unbuckle the harness and swim circles around her and then submerge, staying under for a very long time, Lory thought. She lost track of the time. There was no way for her to bring him up; she could only wait for him. She watched the concentric ripples he'd left in the lake's surface until the water faded to smoothness again. She could feel him down there, somewhere below her, but the water was flat again, motionless. She would try to will him back to the surface, as if raising him with a rope from the bottom of a well, but he'd stay hidden below her.

For A.C., it was dark and yet so deeply safe at the bottom of the lake. But then he would kick for the surface, up to the wavering glimmer of where she was, the glimmer becoming an explosion as he surfaced. He found her trying to pretend she wasn't worried, not even turning her head to look at him.

A.C. would get back into the harness and, like a fish or a whale, he would begin her on her journey again, taking her around and around the lake, leaving a small V behind the canoe. Lory trailed her hand in the water and looked back at the blotted treeline against the night and the restaurant-speckled shore; or she would look out ahead of her at the other shore, equally distant, where there were no lights at all.

With A.C. so close, tied to the end of a rope, pulling her and the boat through the water as if she were a toy, she wanted to stand up and call out, cupping her hands, "I love you." But she stayed seated and let her hand trail in the coolness of the lake. She was not a good swimmer, but she wanted to get in the water with him. She wanted to strip and dive in and swim out to him. He seemed so at ease that Lory would find herself — watching his wet, water-sliding back in the moonlight, the dark water — believing that he had become a sleek sea animal and was no longer a true human, mortal, capable of mortal things.

Occasionally Lory and A.C. went out to the lake in the late afternoon, and she would take a book. Between pages, as he continued to swim, she looked at the tree-line, the shore, all so far away. Sometimes a boat drew near to see if she needed help, but always she waved it away, gave the people in the other boat a cheery, thumbs-up signal. When dusk came, if A.C. had been swimming all afternoon, he would head back to the harbor, side-stroking and looking at her with a slow, lazy smile. But she did not want laziness or slow smiles; she wanted to reach out and hold him.

In the dark harbor he would climb into the boat,

slippery and naked, as she removed her own clothes, pulling off the old sea-green sweater she wore over her swimsuit in the chill night air, then removing the yellow swimsuit itself, and then her earrings, placing all of these things in the bow, out of the way, so that there was nothing, only them. She met him, offering herself as if meat to a wet, slippery animal. They would lie in the bottom of the cool green canoe, hold each kiss, and feel the lake pressing from beneath as they pressed back against it, riding the surface of the water. With the water so very nearly lapping at her skin but not quite — separated only by the canoe's thin shell — Lory felt like some sort of sea creature. One or both of her arms would sometimes hang over the edge of the canoe as they made love, would trail or splash in the water, and often she didn't see why they didn't just get it over with, dive into the lake and never come back to the surface.

Later, they would get up and sit on the wicker bench seat in the stern, side by side, and lean against each other, holding hands.

They would sit in the harbor, those cool nights, wet, steaming slightly from their own heat. Other boats rode slowly into the harbor, idling through the darkness back to shore, their lengths and shapes identifiable by the green and yellow running lights that lined their sides for safety, as they passed through the night, going home. At times it seemed as if one of the pleasure boats were coming right at them, and sometimes one of the boats with bright running lights would pass by — so close that they could see the faces of the people inside.

But they were unobserved. They watched the boats pass and let the night breezes dry their hair, dry the lake water from their bodies so that they felt human once more, and of the earth. They would make love again, invisible to all the other passing boats, all of them full of people who could not see what it was like to be in love.

A.C. and Lory would have coffee at a restaurant on the short drive back — five or six miles from home — on a deck beneath an umbrella like tourists, looking out at Highway 9A. Lory drank her coffee slowly, stirring milk and sugar into it, cup after cup, watching the black liquid turn into swirling, muddy shades of brown. A.C.'s weight was up to three hundred pounds now, more muscle than ever, but she would reach over, smiling, look into his eyes, and grip the iron breadth of his thigh and squeeze it, then pat it and say, "How are you doing, fat boy?"

She felt lake water still inside her, even though they had gone in for a quick cleaning-off swim — A.C. staying right next to her, holding her up in the water with one hand. She felt deliciously wild. They drank coffee for an hour, until their hair was completely dry. Then they drove home, to Louella's dismay and the brothers' looks of happiness, but looks that were somehow a little hurt, a little lost; home to Heck's mild wonderment and interest, looking up from his gin and tonic; home to Lindsay's impatience, for A.C. and Lory would have been gone a long time.

"We're just friends, Mom," Lory would say whenever Louella tried to corner her in the kitchen. "I'm happy, too. See? Look!" She danced, leaped, and kicked her heels together three times, spun around when she landed, then went up on her toes — an odd interpretation of the discus spin that A.C. was trying to learn.

"Well," said Louella, not knowing what to say or do. "Good. I hope so."

·

One morning when A.C. stayed in Glens Falls, he lifted himself from sleep and moved around the basement, examining the old weights, the rowing machines, the rust-locked exercise bikes, and the motionless death-hang of the patched and battered punching bags. A.C. ran his hand over the weights and looked at the flecks of rust that came off on his hands, and thought how the brothers were outlasting the iron and the steel. He stared at the rust in the palm of his hand and smelled the forever-still air that had always been in the basement, air in which John and Jerry had grown up, spindly kids wrestling and boxing, always fighting things, but being part of a family: eating meals together, going to church, teasing their sisters, growing larger, finding directions and interests, taking aim at things. That same air was still down there, as if in a bottle, and it confused A.C. and made him more sure that he was somehow a part of it, a part he did not know about.

He pictured pushing through the confusion, throwing the discus farther and farther, until one day he did the skip-and-glide perfectly. He would be able to spin around once more after that, twice more, and still look up after the throw in time to see the disc flying. It would make the brothers happy, but perhaps then they would not feel that he was a brother anymore.

He trained harder than ever with them, as if it were the greatest of secrets they were giving him. They put their arms around him, walking back from training. Sometimes they teased him, trying to put his great throws in perspective.

"The circumference of the earth at the equator is more than 24,000 miles," Jerry said nonchalantly, looking at his watch as if to see what time it was, as if he had forgotten an appointment. Lory had put him up to it.

She'd given him the numbers to crib on his wrist. "Why, that's over 126,720,000 feet," he'd exclaim.

John looked over at A.C. and said, "How far'd you throw today, A.C.?"

A.C. would toss his head back and laugh a great, happy laugh, the laugh of someone being saved, being thrown a rope and pulled in. He would rather be their brother than anything. He wouldn't do them any harm.

.

Lory and A.C. took Lindsay canoeing on the Battenkill River, over in Vermont. It was almost fall. School was starting soon. Lory stayed close to A.C., held on to his arm, sometimes with both hands. She worried that the fatigue and subsequent depression would be coming on like a returning army, but she smiled thinly, moved through the cool days and laughed, grinning wider whenever their eyes met. Sometimes A.C. would blush and look away, which made Lory grin harder. She would tickle him, tease him; she knew he was frightened of leaving her. She knew he never would.

They drove through the countryside, past fields lined with crumbling stone walls and Queen Anne's lace, with the old canoe on top of the VW. They let Lindsay drive, like a chauffeur. A.C. and Lory had somehow squeezed into the back seat. Now and then Lindsay looked back at them when they kissed, and a crimson blush came into her face, but mostly it was just shy glances at the mirror, trying to see, as if through a telescope, the pleasure that lay ahead of her.

The road turned to white gravel and dust with a clatter and clinking of pebbles, but Lory and A.C. did not notice. They looked like one huge person wedged into the back seat. Sun flashed through the windshield.

It felt good to Lindsay to be driving with the window down, going faster than she ever had. Meadows passed, more Queen Anne's lace, maples, farms, cattle. A.C. reached forward and squeezed the back of Lindsay's neck, startling her, and then began rubbing it. She relaxed, smiled, and leaned her head back. Her red hair on his wrist.

Lindsay drove down the narrow road raising dust, and brilliant goldfinches swept back and forth across the road in front of them, flying out of the cattails, alarmed at the car's speed. Lindsay hit one; it struck the hood and flew straight up above them, sailing back toward the cattails, dead, wings folded, but still a bright yellow color. Lindsay cried "Oh!" and covered her mouth, because neither A.C. nor Lory had seen it. She was ashamed somehow and wanted to keep it a secret.

They stopped for cheeseburgers and shakes at a shady drive-in, in a small Vermont town whose name they'd never heard of. The drive-in was right by the banks of the river, where they would put the canoe in. The river was wide and shallow, cool and clear, and they sat beneath a great red oak and ate. Lindsay was delighted to be with them, but also she could not shake the oddest feeling. Again, the feeling that there was nothing special, that it had been happening all her life, these canoe trips with A.C. and Lory — and that it could just as easily have been John or Jerry sitting with them under the tree. If anything, Lindsay felt a little hollow somehow, and cheated, as if something were missing, because A.C. had shown up only this summer.

Lindsay had never paddled before. She sat backwards and gripped the paddle wrong, like a baseball bat. And Lory did an amazing thing that her sister never understood: she fell out, twice. It was like falling out of a chair. She hadn't even been drinking. Lindsay shrieked. They had water fights.

Lindsay had baked a cake, and they ate it on a small island. When the sisters waded into the cold river to pee, A.C. laughed, turned his back, and made noise against the rocks on the shore.

"Lindsay's jealous," Lory said when they came trudging out of the river. Lindsay swung at her but missed, and fell back into the water.

The sun dried them quickly. Several times A.C. got out of the canoe and swam ahead, pulling them by a rope held in his teeth.

Lory had brought a big jug of wine. They got out and walked up into a meadow and drank from it whenever they became tired of paddling, which was often. At one stop, on the riverbank, Lory ran her fingers through A.C.'s hair. In six years, she would be forty. A crow flew past, low over the river. Farther upstream, they could see trout passing beneath the canoe, could see the bottom of the river, which was deep. Stones lined the river bottom, as if an old road lay beneath them.

On the way home, with A.C. at the wheel, they stopped for more cheeseburgers and had Cokes in the bottle with straws. They kept driving with the windows down. Their faces were not sunburned, but darker.

When A.C., Lory, and Lindsay got home and went into the house, the brothers were immediately happy to see the big man again, as always, but then, like small clouds, something crossed their faces and then vanished again, something unknown, perhaps confused.

•

The day before school started, Lory and A.C. paddled up to the farmhouse in Vermont. They were both sad, as if one of them were leaving and not ever coming back. Lory thought about another year of school. Tired before it even began, she sat on the stone wall with him, her head on his shoulder. He let her stay that way and did not try to cheer her up with stunts or tricks or feats of strength. The cattle in the field grazed right up to the edge of the stone wall, unafraid of Lory and A.C.

He rubbed the back of Lory's neck, held her close against him. He could be kind and tender, he could be considerate and thoughtful, he could even love her, but she wanted something else. He was afraid of this, and knew he was as common as coal in that respect. He also knew he was afraid of leaving, and of being alone.

.

A.C. was running out of money, so he took a paper route. He had no car, so he pulled the papers on a huge scraping rickshaw, fitting himself with a harness to pull it. It had no wheels and was really only a crude travois: two long poles with a sheet of plywood nailed to them, and little guard rails so that he could stack the papers high on it.

He delivered papers in the early afternoon. All through the neighborhoods he trotted, grimacing, pulling a half ton of paper slowly up the small hills, and then, like a creature from the heavens, like some cruel-eyed bird, he swooped down the hills, street gravel and rock rattling under the sled. He shouted and tossed papers like mad, glancing back over his shoulder with every throw to be sure that he was staying ahead of the weight of the sled, which was accelerating, trying to run him down. It was funny, and the people who lived at the bottom of a hill learned to listen for him, loved to watch him, to see if one day he might get caught.

But now it was lonely for A.C., with Jerry in his final year at school, playing football, and John coaching. Lindsay was back in school too, and Heck was still the principal. Only Louella stayed at home.

Usually A.C. finished his paper route by late afternoon, and then he would put the sled in the garage and hose himself off in the back yard, his chest red from where the harness had rubbed, his running shorts drenched with sweat. He'd hold the hose over his head and cool down. Louella would watch from the kitchen window, feeling lonely, but she was also cautious, a mother first.

Dripping, A.C. would turn the water off, coil the hose up, and sit at the picnic table silently, his back turned to the kitchen. Like a dog finished with his duties, he would wait until he could see Lory again, see all the siblings. Louella would watch him for a long time. She just couldn't be sure.

When Lory got home from school, riding on a fresh burst of energy at the idea of seeing him again, A.C. would jump up, shake sprays of water from his wet hair, and run to open the door for her. He kissed her delicately, and she would ask, teasing, "How was your day, dear?" Though it was all working out differently from how she had expected, she was fresher and happier than she had ever been.

•

The children at Lory's school were foul, craven, sunk without hope. She would resurrect one, get a glimmer of interest in one every now and then, but eventually it would all slide back; it had all been false — that faint progress, the improvement in attitude. Sometimes she hit her fist against the lockers after school. The desks with

"I fucked Miss Iron" on them were still there, and the eyes of the male teachers were no better, saying the same thing. She was getting older, older, and each year she wondered if this was the year that the last of her youth would go away. It was a gauntlet, but she needed to stay close to Glens Falls. She had to keep going.

It was like traveling upriver at night in the canoe with him, up through the rapids, only it was like being one of the darkened iron statues rather than her live, loving self. It was like night all the time, this job, and in her dreams of it, there was never any sound, no promise, no future. She was in the wrong place, taking the wrong steps, and she knew — she could feel it as strongly as anything — that it took her too far away from him, teaching at Warrensburg each day, a place of darkness.

She was up until midnight every night, grading papers, preparing lesson plans, reading the barely legible scrawled essays of rage — "I wont to kil my sester, i wont to kil my bruthers" — and then she was up again at four or four-thirty, rousing herself from the sleepy dream of her life. But A.C. was also up by then, making coffee for her.

When they kissed in the morning she'd be wearing a tattered, dingy robe and her owlish reading glasses. His hands would slide under her robe and find her warm beneath the fuzzy cloth. He wanted nothing else for either of them. There could be no improvement. He knew she wanted more, though, that she wanted to keep going.

They would take a short walk right before she left for school. By the time they got back, John and Jerry would be up. Jerry's clock radio played hard rock. John, with no worries, no responsibilities, sorted through the refrigerator for his carton of milk (biceps drawn on it with a

Magic Marker) and got Jerry's carton out (a heart with an arrow through it, and the word "Mom" inside the heart). The brothers stood around and drank, swallowing the milk in long, cold gulps.

.

Watching A.C. and Lory grow closer was, to Louella, like the pull of winter, or like giving birth. Always, she thought about the one she had lost. Twenty years later, she had been sent a replacement. She wanted to believe that. She had not led a martyr's life, but she had worked hard, and miracles did happen.

It was true, she realized. She could make it be true by wanting it to be true.

She looked out her kitchen window at him, sitting at the picnic table with his back to her, facing the garden, the late-season roses. Sun came through the window, and she could see hummingbirds fly into the back yard, lured by the sweetness of the nectar she had put in the feeders.

Louella watched A.C. look around at the hummingbirds, staring at them for the longest time, like a simple animal. The birds were dancing flecks of color, flashes of shimmering emerald and cobalt. Louella saw a blur of orange in the garden, the cat racing across the yard, up onto the picnic table, then leaping into the air, legs outstretched. She saw the claws, and like a ballplayer the cat caught one of the hummingbirds in midair, came down with it, and tumbled and rolled.

Louella watched as A.C. ran to the cat, squeezed its neck gently, and lifted the limp hummingbird from the cat's mouth. The cat shivered, shook, and ran back into the garden. A.C. set the limp hummingbird down on the picnic table. The other hummingbirds were gone.

Louella went into the back yard. The little bird lay still with its eyes shut, a speck of blood on its throat like a tiny ruby. The glitter of its green back like scales.

"That damn cat," Louella said, but as they watched, the hummingbird began to stir, ruffled its feathers, looked around, and flew away.

·

Each morning after the others had left, A.C. would sit at the picnic table a bit longer. Then he would come inside and tell Louella that he was going to Vermont for a while. Always, politely, he asked her if she needed anything, or if she cared to go with him for the ride, and always she refused, saying she had things to do. Always, afterward, she wished she had said yes, wondered what it would be like, wondered what his stone farmhouse looked like. But there were boundaries to be maintained; she could not let go and say yes. So A.C. would lift the canoe over his head and walk through the neighborhood, out across the main road and down to the river, leaving her alone.

What A.C. was working on in Vermont was a barn, for throwing the discus during the winter months. He wanted to perfect his throw, to make John and Jerry happy. He had no more money left, so he ripped down abandoned barns, saving even the nails from the old boards. He built his barn in the woods, on the side of the hill behind his farmhouse. It was more like a bowling alley than anything.

He had planned it to be 300 feet long. He climbed high into the trees to nail on the tall roof that would keep the snow out. There was not enough wood to build sides for the barn; mostly it was like a tent, a long, open-walled shed. He had built up the sides with stones about three feet high to keep the drifts from blowing in. It would be cold, but it would be free of snow.

He cut the trees down with an ax, to build the throwing lane, and then cut them into lengths to be dragged away. He was building a strip of empty space in the heart of the woods; it ran for a hundred yards and then stopped. He kept it a secret from the whole family, and was greatly pleased with its progress as the fall went on.

The air inside the throwing room felt purified, denser somehow. It had the special scents of the woods. He burned all the stumps, leveled the ground with a shovel and hoe, and made a throwing ring out of river stones. The rafters overhead reminded him of the church he'd gone to once with the Irons: the high ceiling, the beams, keeping the hard rains and snows out, protecting them, but also distancing them from what it was they were after.

He would work on the barn all morning, leave in time to get home and do his paper route, and still be back at the house before anyone else got there. Sometimes Louella would be out shopping or doing other errands. He would sit at the picnic table and wait for the sound of Lory's car.

.

Feathery snow fell on the Hudson highlands on the third of October, a Friday night. They were all walking to the movie theater in the mall, A.C. and Lory holding hands, Lindsay running ahead of them. It was too early for real snow.

The brothers were as full of spirit as they had been all year. It was as if they were fourteen. They danced, did their discus spins in crowded places, ending their imaginary releases with wild shouts that drew some spectators and scared others away, then all three of them spun and whooped — John's and Jerry's spins still more polished than A.C.'s, but A.C.'s impressive also, if for no reason other than his great size. Soon there was a large audience, clapping and cheering as if they were Russian table dancers. (A.C. pictured it being late spring still, or early summer, before he had met them: back when he was still dancing with the cows on his back, a sport he had enjoyed, and which he secretly missed, though the brothers had asked him to stop doing it, saying it would throw his rhythm off. He missed the freedom of it, the lack of borders and rules, but did not want to hurt their feelings, did not want them to know he thought discus throwing was slightly inferior, so he'd done as they said, though still, he missed dancing and whirling with the cattle over his shoulders.)

Lory shrieked and hid her eyes with her hands, embarrassed, and Lindsay blushed her crimson color, but was petrified, unable to move, and she watched them, amazed as always. Lory's fingers were digging into Lindsay's arm; Lindsay smiled bravely through her embarrassment, and was happy for Lory. Everyone around them in the mall kept clapping and stamping their feet, while outside, the first snow came down.

.

A.C. gave the money from the paper route to Louella and Heck, and as he made more money, he tried to give that to them as well, but they wouldn't hear of it. So he bought things and gave them to Lory. He bought whatever he saw, if he happened to be thinking about her: a kitten, bouquets of flowers, jewelry, an NFL football, a smoked turkey.

She was flattered and excited the first few times he

brought something home, but soon became alarmed at the volume of things, and eventually asked him to stop. Then she had to explain to him what she really wanted, what really made her happy, and he was embarrassed, felt a fool for not having realized it before, for having tried to substitute. It was like throwing the discus from his hip rather than with the spin, he realized.

They went out in the canoe again that Saturday night, on Lake George. It was a still night at first, calm and chilly, and the full moon was so bright they could see the shore, even from far out on the water. They could see each other's face, each other's eyes; it was like some dream-lit daylight, hard and blue and silver, with the sound of waves lapping against the side of their small boat. They were cold, but they undressed anyway. They wanted to get close, as close as they could; they wanted to be all there was in the world, the only thing left.

He covered her with the blanket they had brought, and kept her warm with that and with himself. After making love to her he fell asleep, dreaming, in the warmth of the blanket and the roll of the boat, that he was still in her, that they were still loving, and that they always would be.

"You were smiling," she said when he woke around midnight. She'd been watching him all night. She'd held him, too, sometimes pressing him so tightly against her breast that she was sure he'd wake up, but he had slept on. "What were you smiling about?"

"You," he said sleepily. "I was thinking about you."

It was the right answer. She was so happy.

.

One weekend, Lory's school had a Halloween dance. A girl had been raped after the dance last year, and several of the teachers' cars had had their tires slashed and their radio antennas snapped. A small fire had been set inside the school and had scorched the walls. Lory was chaperoning this year. She went up there with John and Jerry and A.C., and stayed near them the whole time.

The brothers dwarfed Lory like bodyguards; she was almost hidden whenever she was in their midst. The young thugs and bullies did not attempt to reach out from the crowd and squeeze her breasts, as they sometimes did on dares, and the male teachers, married and unmarried, treated her with respect. The four of them sat in the bleachers and watched the dance, listening to the loud music until midnight. There was no mischief, and they were relieved when it was time to go.

They felt almost guilty, driving home to warmth and love. They rode in silence, thinking their own thoughts, back down to Glens Falls, whose lights they could see below, not twinkling as if with distance but shining steadily, a constant glow, because they were so close.

•

Geese, heading south late in the year, stragglers. A.C. worked on his barn during the mild sunny days of November. He could feel more snow coming, could feel it the way an animal can. The hair on his arms and legs was getting thicker, the way it had in Colorado in past falls. The barn reminded him of the one that had been out there — the hay barn. That was where she had done it.

The throwing barn was almost finished. It was narrow, so his throws would have to be accurate. There could be no wildness, or he would wreck the place he had built. He would teach himself to throw straight.

He finished the barn in mid-November, as the big flakes arrived, the second snow of the season. Now the snows that came would not go away, not until the end of winter. He brought the brothers up to see the barn, to show them how they could keep training together, how they could keep throwing all through the winter, even with snow banked all around them, and they were delighted.

"This is the best year of my life," Jerry said unexpectedly.

A.C. bought a metal detector, and when throws did not travel perfectly straight — the barn was only thirty feet wide — the brothers and A.C. had to search in the snow, listening for the rapid signal that told them they were getting near. They used old metal discs now, which flew two or three feet farther in the cold air. The brothers ate more than ever, and trained harder.

There was a stone wall at the end of the barn, the 300-foot mark, stacked all the way to the rafters and chinked with mud and sand and grass. A.C. had lodged a discus in it once, had skipped a few of them against its base. Hitting that mark was magical, unimaginable; it required witchcraft, an alteration of reality.

It took the brothers and A.C. about sixty seconds to walk 300 feet. A minute away — and unobtainable, or almost.

Sometimes the throws went too far off into the woods, and the discs were lost for good. Other times, they went too high and crashed through the rafters, like violent cannonballs, cruel iron seeking to destroy.

"Forget it," John would say gruffly whenever A.C. threw outside the barn. They'd hear the snapping, tearing sound of branches being broken and then the *whack!* of the discus striking a tree trunk. John would already be reaching for another disc, though, handing it to him. "Come on, come on, shake it off. Past history. Over and done with. Shake it off."

Past history. No harm done. These were sweet words to A.C. His eyes grew moist. He wanted to believe that. He wanted to make good this time.

·

As the winter deepened, they set their goals harder and farther. John and Jerry wanted to throw 221 feet, and A.C. wanted to be able to throw 300 feet on any given throw, at will.

And he wanted Lory. He wanted to build fences, to take care, protect. Sometimes while everyone was at school, Louella would decide that she just couldn't keep away any longer. She would challenge herself to be brave, to accept him without really knowing whether he was hers or not. She would ride in the canoe with him up to the barn, to watch him throw. She had come over to his side, and believed in him, and she did that. Louella wanted to know about his past, but A.C. simply wouldn't tell her.

A.C. built a fire for Louella in the barn, and she sat on a stump and sipped coffee while he threw. His spin was getting better. It was an imitation of her sons', she could tell, but it was starting to get some fluidity to it, some life, some creativity. Louella enjoyed watching him train. His clumsiness did not worry her, because she could tell he was working at it and overcoming it. She was even able to smile when the discus soared up through the rafters, letting a sprinkle of snow pour into the barn from above — yet another hole punched through the roof, one more hole of many, the snow sifting down like fine powder.

They were alarming, those wild throws, but she found herself trusting him. Secretly she liked the wild throws: she was fascinated by the strength and force behind them, the utter lack of control. It was like standing at the edge of a volcano, looking down. She moved a little closer to the fire. She was fifty-eight, and was seeing things she'd never seen before, feeling things she'd never felt. Life was still a mystery. He had made her daughter happy again.

"Keep your head back," Louella would caution whenever she saw that his form was too terribly off. "Keep your feet spread. Your feet were too close together." She knew enough about form to tell how it differed from her other sons'.

.

The whole family came for Thanksgiving: cousins and moved-away aunts, little babies, uncles and nieces. Everything flowed. A.C. was a good fit; it was as if he'd always been there. Passing the turkey, telling jokes, teasing Lindsay about a boyfriend; laughter and warmth inside the big house.

The roads iced over. There was the sound of studded snow tires outside, and of clanking chains. Football all day on television, and more pie, more cider. Then Thanksgiving passed and they were on into December, the Christmas season, with old black-and-white movies on television late at night and Lory on her holiday break from school. Everyone was home, and he was firmly in their center, her center.

He was in a spin of love and asked her to marry him. "Yes," she said, laughing, remembering last year's sadness and the crazy lost hope of it, never dreaming or knowing that he had been out there, moving toward her.

In her dreams, in the months preceding the wedding, she saw images of summer, of June coming around again. She and her mother stood in a large field, with cattle grazing near the trees. In the field were great boulders and fieldstones left over from another age, a time of glaciers and ice, of great floods.

And in the dream, she and her mother leaned into the boulders, rolling them, moving them out of the field, making the field pure and green. They built a stone wall out of the boulders, all around the field, and some of them were too large to move. Lory gritted her teeth and pushed harder, straining, trying to move them all. Then she would wake up and be by his side, by his warmth, and realize that she had been pushing against him, trying to get him out of bed. That could not be done, and she'd laugh, put her arms around as much of him as she could, and bury her face in him. Then she would get up after a while, unable to return to sleep.

She'd dress, put on her snow boots, go to the garage, and pick up one of the discuses, holding it with both hands, feeling the worn smoothness, the coldness, and the magic of it — magic, Lory believed, because he had touched it. Certain that no one was watching, that no one could ever find out, she would go into the front yard, bundled up in woolens and a parka, and under the blue cast of the streetlight she'd crouch and then whirl, spinning around and around, and throw the discus as far as she could, in whatever direction it happened to go. She'd shout, almost roar, and watch it sink into the soft new snow, jumping up and down afterward when she threw well and was pleased with her throw.

Then she would wade out to where she had seen the discus disappear, kneel down, and dig for it with her hands. She'd carry it back to the garage, slip it into the box with the others, and finally she'd be able to sleep, growing warm again in bed with him.

In the spring, before the wedding, after the snows melted and the river began to warm — the river in which A.C. had first seen and swum up to his brothers — he began to swim again, but with Lory this year.

A.C. would fasten a rope to the harness around his chest and tie the other end of it to the bumper of her car before leaping into the river from a high rock and being washed down through the rapids.

Then he would swim upriver until his shoulders ached, until even he was too tired to lift his head, and was nearly drowning. Lory would leap into the car then, start it, and ease up the hill, pulling him like a limp wet rag through the rapids he'd been fighting, farther up the river until he was in the stone-bottomed shallows. She'd park the car, set the emergency brake, jump out, and run back down to get him.

Like a fireman, she'd pull him the rest of the way out of the river, splashing knee-deep in the water, helping him up, putting his arm around her tiny shoulders. Somehow they'd stagger up into the rocks and trees along the shore. He'd lie on his back and gasp, looking up at the sky and the tops of trees, and smelling the scent of pines. They would lie in the sun, drenched, exhausted, until their clothes were almost dry, and then they would back the car down and do it again.

He liked being saved. He needed her. And she needed him. Closer and closer she'd pull him, reeling in the wet rope, dragging him up on shore, bending over and kissing his wet lips until his eyes fluttered, bringing him back to life every time.

PLATTE RIVER

The man must not drink of the running streams, the living waters, who is not prepared to have all nature reborn in him — to suckle monsters.

— THOREAU, *August 1851 journal*

Shaw used to be a model and is still beautiful, fierce and timid both, like a coyote or a wild dog — more beautiful, in that way, than when she modeled. Harley is strange looking, as plain as butter, huge, and believes in his heart, with his ragged dress, his half beard, his falling-out hair, and his badger's temper, that he makes Shaw feel older, less beautiful, less whole. Less than what she used to be. Harley tells Shaw this, to hear her deny it, and she does deny it, and keeps denying it until the time she packs to move out, saying that she feels older, no longer beautiful, no longer whole — but that it's not Harley's doing.

Harley's forty-one. Shaw is thirty-eight. Old enough to have lived full lives, and yet they have not even started.

She takes her time leaving this time. Usually she bolts in the night, hitchhiking, since they have only one old truck between them, which runs infrequently. But this time Shaw has told Harley of her fears, her feelings, calmly, matter-of-factly, rather than just fleeing. She's already met with the bank officer in the small town nearest where they live. It's an hour's drive down out of Canada, along a one-lane cliff road. Shaw and Harley have a mailbox in northern Montana, but they live up over the line, ten miles into Canada, on an old logging road. Their house is an abandoned hunting lodge, large and airy, with the stuffed heads of deer and elk, moose and bear, staring down at them from the walls — ancient heads from animals shot fifty and sixty years ago. It's such a fairy-tale existence, Harley thinks, with the big, stone-circled fireplaces, the cavernous bedroom — everything oversized, as if a giant had once lived in the lodge — that he often thinks they've died and are living some sort of afterlife, separate from the real world.

Then Harley realizes that's the problem, that he loves the empty, echoing, ringing feeling, but that Shaw is terrified of it.

She used the silk scarves that she paints as collateral. She stretches the silk between sawhorses in the back yard, and then, wearing a big straw hat to protect her face from the thin mountain sun, she paints abstract patterns across the silks before hemming the edges and sewing them into things — scarves mostly, but also skirts, blouses, ties. The car she's taken the loan on is an old Subaru. Shaw parks it in the back yard and paints that, too — autumn red and lichen green, swirling.

"I need a car that'll get around in the snow," she tells Harley. It's April, the month it always is when she leaves, right after the long winter. Like an animal coming to its senses, Harley thinks; like an animal waking up.

It's late April and she's talking about snow. That

means she'll be gone longer than two or three weeks, he thinks. Till November at least. Maybe longer.

.

Shaw cries sometimes after they make love. Harley asks her why.

"I just think about how sad it's going to make you when I leave," she says.

They still make love often — in the woods, with tiger stripes of sunlight falling across their bodies and the snow-melt river hurtling past. Shaw gazes into Harley's eyes during love — into the back of his eyes, into his *cells,* Harley thinks — but then she bursts into tears the second it is over, and it's the end of beauty, and nothing but semen, cooling.

It's a restlessness. Nothing specific, but it's strong.

She remembers how he was when he hurt his knees and had to leave the league — how they wouldn't let him play football anymore, how much he needed her then, how they moved up to these woods. Shaw can leave the lover part of the relationship — that's her choice, she feels. But leaving the friendship part, just cutting loose and drifting away from that, too . . . She feels guilty, almost to the point of feeling anchored — drowning, going down at sea with chains wrapped around her body, around her neck. Fish swimming through her hair.

It's why she takes so long to leave. She's never left a friend before. His steadiness, trustworthiness . . . If he were handsome, she thinks, she would hate him rather than love him, for trying to hold her there with that. But she can't explain this to him. He thinks she's saying it to make him feel better, preparing him for when she does it: leaves.

This *planned* leaving — it's new, it's curtains, it's the end of the line, he thinks. The way Shaw's applying for that loan, the way she packs carefully, each day, one more box — buttons, fabric, paints, brushes, winter clothes. It's nothing like the usual, once a month, mad leavings whereupon Shaw and Harley would get in a shrieking fight. Names would be called, and called back, and Shaw, despondent, would burn her bridges, race out into the night, and, if it was snowing, flounder across the field, running high-kneed through the drifts, across the meadow, and down the lonely, icy road. Harley would rush upstairs and, in his bull rage, his anguish at having lost her, at having not been good enough — at having been baited into a fight rather than being gentle and letting the name-calling drift past him — would begin butting his head against the wall of the log cabin, bellowing with pain.

This, in the winter.

When he had finished beating his head against the wall, when he was able finally to feel the pain subside, the drumming blood-pulse between his ears and through his head slow down, then the giant three-story cabin would be immense in its emptiness. Harley would remember how short life was, but how long it was, too. With his bad knees he'd hobble down the stairs, around and around their boxy spiral and out the front door, running now as if for his life, believing that each time she leaves will surely be the last, that she will not calm down, will not return or allow herself to be caught but will keep running, down the road and then off into the woods, up over Roderick Buttes and then higher, over Lost Horse Mountain and into the next valley, and then to the one beyond that, running to Alaska, perhaps.

They race through the woods: always, it seems, at

night, as if there were some dark biochemical stirring when the light fades and the woods around them grow gloomy and dark. Shaw bolts from the center of the empty road she's walking down when she hears him coming, bolts into the woods, into the trees. And like a hound after a fox, like a wolf chasing a deer, Harley runs after her. They both zig and zag, leaping logs, running through the forest. When Harley catches up with her (feeling, strangely, a terror even greater than hers when he corners her — exhausted, both of them panting, Shaw with her back up against a stand of trees, half bent over, the way a moose will do when bayed by a pack of wolves), he doesn't try to calm her with words, with promises or apologies, or ask for forgiveness. Instead, he picks her up (he doesn't feel her fists as she struggles and tosses her head back and forth, finally going limp, crying, her hair tangled and hiding her face) and carries her out of the woods and back up the deserted gravel road to their cabin, to what used to be their cabin — theirs, not simply hers or his — and to what Harley hopes will be theirs once again.

He lays her — if it's fall, or winter, or even cold spring — in front of the fireplace, which is always flickering and hissing with low coals. Harley covers her with a blanket. She turns her head away from him and stares into the fire, hating him, hating everything, knowing only that she feels trapped and must run, hating him for trying to control her.

Bears in the autumn night, or winter's forty-below blizzards, it makes no difference. When Shaw wants to run, she runs.

After the sleepless night, things are better, though rocky for a couple of days, rocky and raw. Shaw paints new scarves — down in the basement if it's cold out, or in the back yard if it's late spring or summer or fall — fierce-colored abstract slashes on shimmering silk, teardrops and razor stripes of unheralded colors, colors exceeding even the golds and blues and fireweed reds of the country's late summer. She paints bending over the silks, straight-lipped, furious, about to cry — paints like a madwoman, unsure if she wants to stay or leave, wanting to leave for her next journey but afraid to, and furious, no longer at big dumb Harley for trying to hold her but at herself, for being frightened. And Harley feels as if he's used the last faint glimmers of her love for him as a lure with which to bring her back, with which to hold her one last time. Always, he feels it's the last time.

Later in the day, if the afternoon sun is warmer, Shaw hangs her newly painted scarves on the side of the barn, tacks them to the boards as if they're animal hides. They flutter brightly in the wind, four or five of them at a time, so bright and shimmering that to anyone passing (though no one does) it would, *must*, seem as if everything's right, as if there's only peace, as if there's no restlessness in the world.

·

This time, Shaw packs the boxes slowly. And she thoroughly cleans the house — scrubbing it, even the farthest corners, to preface her departure — moving methodically, logically, gathering her courage steadily so that it will last. This time it terrifies Harley. He knows that empty-cabin feeling is rising to meet him again, and that he won't be able to do anything about it.

If she doesn't run, how can he catch her?

Harley feels his power being drained from him. He feels Shaw growing stronger. The scarves flap and dry in the wind, as if they, too, are trying to take flight. They, and their fluttering message of freedom, are infinitely more brilliant than an aging, predictable Harley.

.

While Shaw goes down to Montana and Idaho to scout out work and a new place to live, Harley flies to northern Michigan to visit an old friend and teammate of his, Willis, who was never drafted, who never played for money, but perhaps should have. He had been a small, churlish running back nicknamed "the Wolverine," whom Harley spent three years blocking for, protecting, when they went to college in Ohio.

Willis — the Wolverine — teaches English. He's not erudite, but he learned the same plays — *Hamlet, The Tempest, The Cherry Orchard* — over and over again, so he can present them to the burning young students, the best students in art from around the country, in a way that is acceptable to them. They like the Wolverine's dark looks, his distant, permanent scowl, which often leads people to mistake him for a brooding artist, but which is really simply the scowl of a wolverine. They like his short, wide, muscular, artist's body: to them he looks like a paragraph.

It's sort of a scam that the Wolverine has been able to hire his old blocking buddy to come out to the art school and talk about football: fifteen hundred dollars for the weekend. Things are so crazy at home that Harley would do it for free, just to get out of the house, but he's glad for the money. He thinks how if he were married, he would give the government half for taxes and the other half for alimony, after the divorce, leaving him nothing — nothing — for his work.

It's wicked and greedy, he knows, to think this way, but it's what he's thinking, and he can't help it. It gives

him a small, stupid solace — for once — that Shaw
wouldn't marry him, back when he asked.

·

Willis picks Harley up at the Traverse City airport late
in the afternoon. Harley's been traveling for a day and a
night to get out of the woods: driving out of Canada,
slipping across into the States, and on down to Spokane.
He had to take a staggering number of cross-connections
and route-around flights, each one moving him, albeit
obliquely, closer to his destination, to the Wolverine's
own small lair, also on the Canadian line. Harley made
the last leg of the journey in a hydroplane, his big knees
pummeling the seat of the passenger in front of him as
they crossed the choppy air in that ancient plane.

Willis trots out to the runway to meet him when the
plane lands, and the two men exchange high fives, bump
asses, twirl and dance the way they did fifteen years
earlier, with no sadness or parody whatsoever. All the
people in the small airport, even the pilots, look down
and watch the two bulky men — one tall, one short —
bump and shimmy on the runway.

It's windy, gusting up to fifty miles an hour: it's still
winter in northern Michigan. The wind catches the Wolverine's hat, lifts it from his head, and tumbles it down
the runway. Spirited away, it's moving fifty, sixty yards
at a clip, farther and farther out of reach, gone so fast
that they don't even consider chasing it. The two men
just observe it for a second, and then laugh and head for
the terminal with their arms around each other's shoulders, Harley limping slightly from the day's cramped
travels.

They drive the last fifteen miles to the campus in
Willis's rusted-out Toyota. Harley can see the road rushing beneath them through holes in the floorboard, can

hear the wind whistling up into the car. It looks like winter: pearl-gray sky, bare trees, and patches of dirty snow.

Fifteen hundred dollars, Harley thinks. He feels like he shouldn't have gone off and left Shaw. It's green already down low in their valley, in southern Alberta and northern Montana. He tries to think of something else.

"How're you doing?" Willis asks. "The trip — you look rough."

"It's good to be here," Harley says. "It's real good to see you. But I feel like I'm slumming. I feel like they just want to gawk. I mean, none of them will even have heard of me. I feel like they just want to say, 'We touched an ex–football player. We had a hunk of meat speaking on our little campus this week. We're different, we're *out there*. Other art schools bring in fey poets and piano tuners, but we bring in meat, to broaden our horizons.'" Harley picks at his fingernails. "I feel like they just want to gawk," he says again.

Willis nods, then shrugs. "Some of them will," he says. "But they're good kids. Give them a break."

They turn off the main road and drive down a hard dirt road that runs through a forest of bare-limbed birches. They come out of the bottom and drive up into pines. Harley can see a lake through the trees.

"Just talk about football," Willis says. "Talk about what you know. These kids are insatiable. They want to know about everything — I mean everything. Give them the Nietzsche stuff, the van Gogh, about how one must be one's own horse. Or that one that Coach Shea used to give us."

Harley smiles. "*Hit, hit, hit,*" he says, looking out the window. The lake is whitecapping. Trees line it all around the shore. It's a large lake.

"We'll go fishing tonight, if that's okay with you,"

Willis says. "Me and you and a couple of the other teachers. They're good guys and want to meet you."

The wind's rocking the little car. Harley looks over at Willis, the Wolverine, and it's not like they're kids anymore, or even young men. They can see the age in each other. But it's still a good feeling, an exciting one, a new one — as if there's still much country to be covered and plenty of strength left with which to cover it.

"Steelhead," Willis says. "We'll have some burgers and some pie and coffee over at my house. I want you to meet my wife and little girl. Then we'll go out to the Platte River and catch some steelhead. I've got all the gear you'll need."

"Super," says Harley, delighted to have something to take his mind off things. He imagines Shaw filling one more box, even at that moment: arranging it neatly, packing it and repacking it, getting it just right. "Wonderful," Harley says.

They come to the guest cottage where Harley will be staying. It's yellow with fading green trim, and is set back on a hill among the pines, looking out at the lake, which is visible as a glint of blue through the trees. Willis gives Harley the key to the cottage and lets him out at the bottom of the hill.

"This place is great," Harley says.

"God, it's great to see you," Willis says, grabbing Harley's hand and squeezing it.

Harley remembers all the enemy tacklers he cut down trying to protect Willis, trying to keep them away, and grins back. "It's great to be here."

"I'll pick you up in an hour," Willis says. "I'll go get you a license and get everything rounded up — that'll give you time to freshen up. We'll wade where the river goes into the lake. Shit, it's great that you're here," he says, shaking Harley's hand once more.

Harley climbs out of the car, shoulders his overnight bag, waves goodbye, then walks up the steps of the cottage. Harley can hear the wind slapping the water against the rocky shore; even when he's inside, he can hear that sound.

It's a tiny cottage: no television, no electricity, just a bed, a desk, and a bathroom. He sits down on the bed and looks out the brightly washed window at the lake and listens to it. The room is lonely in its smallness. There's nothing to do but watch the lake. It's Shaw who should be here, not him, he thinks. These kids don't want to know about football.

There's no one out. Harley imagines that they are all in a cafeteria somewhere, talking about flutes and poetry and vases — olden shit. He gazes at the water for a long time. The sun through the window and the sound of the waves is making him sleepier than he's ever been, but as an exercise in discipline he tries to stay awake, refuses to lie down, not even for a minute or two. Finally, as if it is the thing he has been watching for, he sees another person. It's a young woman walking her yellow Labrador on a leash. She's walking slowly with her head down — a sad woman, Harley thinks. He watches her until she disappears into the trees.

He's napping hard when he hears a knock on the door. In his dream Harley was hitting his head against the cabin wall again, faster and faster, after Shaw had left again, but then he hears Willis's voice — "Hey, Harley, it's me" — and Willis is poking his head in the door, saying, "Wake up, Heine Man." It's one of Harley's nicknames from college, due to the wideness of his girth. Harley sits up slowly, wondering how long Shaw's been gone and wondering where he is. For a moment it seems that his life with Shaw and the dream of banging his head against the wall are what's real, and that Willis, with his head halfway through the door, grinning, and the afterlife-lulling washes of the waves, the heavy forest right outside the window, are what the dream is. The sun is down behind the trees, the light is leaving the room — the forest is becoming dark — and Harley's chilled. He wants to be home, but fifteen hundred dollars is fifteen hundred dollars, and he rises from the bed, lumbers into the bathroom. He splashes water on his face and they're off, out of the cottage and into Willis's car.

·

The Wolverine seems to be a little more fidgety, a little more restless, than Harley remembered from school, but he decides that's to be expected: it's late in the winter, and spring's long overdue. Maybe Willis is unhappy, too, being a jock among the effetes.

"It's my tenth anniversary, man," Willis says, grinning almost maniacally, holding the steering wheel with both hands. Harley notices how tense Willis's shoulders are, how his trapezius muscles seem to be riding a little higher than usual, and remembers the masseuse who used to come to their dorm after games at their small Ohio college, and how, in the pros, there had not been such a masseuse, and how he'd been disappointed by that fact. Dixie, he thinks, trying to remember. Harley feels like a fossil. This was all so long ago. He gets the feeling that "Congratulations" isn't the thing Willis wants him to say, but he says it anyway. It's all there is to say.

"She won't be at your talk tomorrow," Willis says apologetically. "She's got that winter depression thing." He holds his hand out, making it flutter like a crippled bird. Willis says it with concern, but the way he's making his hand dip and dive strikes Harley as funny, and he laughs but then is mortified to see Willis scowl — it's no laughing matter for him — and the subject is dropped. Harley stares out the window, his face crimson, and in the late-day light watches for deer running through the forest, the way they do back home.

"This teaching," Willis says after a while. "I've been doing it fifteen years." Harley looks over at him and thinks that Willis still looks to be in okay shape — nothing like he was in college, but still probably stronger and faster than ninety-eight percent of the rest of the world, and wasn't that enough after fifteen years? You're either there on the peak of perfection, the peak of strength, Harley thinks, or you're not.

"I just feel like *driving,*" Willis says. "I just feel like letting you out at the house and *going* somewhere — anywhere. Just driving for days."

Harley nods and looks at the woods race past. They're almost at Willis's house, which is at the other end of the lake. They ride the rest of the way in silence. Willis is wrapped up in the idea of a long flight, his eyes luminous with the thought of it, and Harley, picking at his thumbnail, is trying to think of what he'll say tomorrow, trying to figure out a way to take home the fifteen hundred with pride rather than guilt. Trying to figure out why Shaw's unhappy, why she wants to leave when she doesn't seem to have anything to run to — trying to figure out what's wrong with him that makes her want to run away. Harley's read and heard about the biological clock, but to him sometimes it's more like a fuse. He wonders, could it be that?

"Jack and Lois'll be there," Willis says. "Jack teaches with me. They're great. Jack's funny, a nice guy." He clears his throat. "And Nick and Shellie will be there.

Nick Bozaine. He's a poet. Jack and Nick and you and me are going fishing. Jack's a poet too, but he's normal. Nick's, well, Nick is . . ." Willis flutters his hand again and looks at Harley with what almost seems to be warning, or apology.

"Nick's a sweet guy, a prince of a guy, the rarest man there is — but he gets sad," Willis says. "He's manic-depressive, and he's in the middle of a big one right now." Willis shakes his head. "He tried to kill himself once."

"How," says Harley, dully.

"Garage," says Willis. "Left the car running in the garage one winter and lay down in the front seat. Wrapped up in a blanket and went to sleep. His ex-wife — his first one — came home and got him to the hospital." Willis sighs as he pulls into the driveway. "Maybe my best friend here on campus. Sweetest man who ever walked the face of the earth. Been married four times and he's only thirty-five years old."

Willis's house, which he is renting from the academy, is beautiful, charming. It's nestled in the trees, off by itself with toys strewn around it. When they get out of the car — bats flitting through the trees in the heavy dusk — a golden retriever leaps across the yard and rolls itself, in a crude cross-body block, at Harley's feet. He bends down to pat it. There's a Hula-Hoop in the yard, and some little girls' bicycles and a deflated soccer ball. The porch light is on. A few mayflies bruise themselves against its glow. Willis pauses, going up the steps, and watches the hatch with a fisherman's eyes, still imagining himself traveling — somewhere in the West, perhaps.

When Harley steps into the house, he's frightened for a second because all he can see is a great wall of water, gunmetal gray, rolling toward him. It's like he's stepped off the edge of the world, but then he realizes it's just a huge bay window, the largest he's ever seen — the entire back wall of the house is one immense sheet of glass, jutting over the lake. Seated on couches in the foreground, as if before a big movie screen, are all the people he will meet: Jack and Lois, Nick and Shellie, and Claudia — Willis's wife — and their little girl, Jamie.

Harley looks at them, his pulse still racing, as Claudia turns and rises, comes forward to greet him, to shake his hand. She's smiling weakly but genuinely, and Harley feels guilty, intruding upon her personal illness at the end of the long winter, forcing her to be cheerful. Jamie comes flying across the room, launches herself at Harley's bulk as if trying to tackle him, and gives him a thigh hug.

"You're Daddy's *friend*," she cries, swinging around Harley's tree legs. "I am Jamie!"

Then Harley meets Jack, who is sturdy (but not as sturdy as Willis or, Harley thinks, himself), bearded, and red-faced, as if from having drunk a bottle of schnapps. Jack's as cheerful and yet quiet as a drugstore Santa Claus, and Lois, who is a fashion model, one-quarter Cherokee, is as cheerful and honest and straight as Jack. Another model, Harley thinks. Then he meets Nick, who's ghost-white pale, a kind of after-long-winter pale, tall, and gaunt. He offers a faint, friendly smile as he rises to shake Harley's hand. Nick's vivacious wife, Shellie, who's perhaps an inch or two over five feet, looks strong, furious with energy and ideas, as she shakes Harley's hand, too.

Claudia has made cherry pie, and she cuts into it and serves it to the men and to Lois. Shellie's dieting, though she's as tiny as a fairy already. Everyone stands eating the pie while night falls over the lake. They are all within a few years of being forty, and Willis can't go wrong with the music he puts on the CD player: the Stones, Dylan, the Eagles. Their tastes in music are the most predictable thing about them.

Nick's eating anything he can get his hands on — to keep from talking, Harley can tell — loading up on chips, olives, pie, cookies. The women are talking among themselves. Willis stands by the stereo and looks exhausted, but pleased, and Jack's eyes are shiny as he talks to Nick and Willis about the year's luck thus far in steelhead fishing, and about how frigid and windy it'll be, and about how late they'll be out, all night, and how he hopes they'll catch fish tonight.

Harley tries to listen, grinning, but Jamie's pulling on his arm, wanting to show him her room: her hamster, her aquarium, pictures of her friends. Imperceptibly, he feels Shaw slipping off the side of an iceberg, two thousand miles away — calving, he remembers it's called — feels their lives together cleaving and sloughing away, falling over the cliff, landing with a giant splash in the night, sinking. He would have given ten years of his life for her to be with him tonight, to have seen the lake rolling toward that bay window, and to meet all these people, these friends of the Wolverine.

Jamie's selling raffle tickets in conjunction with her school circus. Harley asks if he'll win an elephant, and Jamie squeals, falls over on her bed laughing and shrieking. Her eyes are rolling back with hyperactivity, and Harley knows enough about children to realize he's not making Claudia's job any easier, that Jamie's got to start calming down for the end of the day rather than getting wound up. But he can't help it, he wants to see how much energy this child has, and he sits down on the bed beside her and says, "A gorilla. I want to win a gorilla to take back on the plane with me." Jamie shrieks even louder and sits up, pummeling her legs against the side of the bed. Her face is red with laughter, and tears are in her eyes. She's clapping her hands, she's so delighted to have a new friend, and Claudia calmly sticks her head in the door and gives Jamie a nice mother look, and whispers, "Ssshh. Calm *down*. Ssshhh."

Harley wonders how long Claudia's had the winter sickness. He wonders if it will go away quickly, with the first sunny warm day, or gradually, and he wonders if there are ever cases of it where, one year, it doesn't go away at all.

"The pie was delicious," Harley says, which is the truth. He wants to tell her something else, something significant (he thinks of his lecture tomorrow, and gropes — this is a woman, a beautiful woman, and he does not think she would appreciate the old words of his and Willis's coach, *Hit, hit, hit*), but the pie is all he can come up with. The pie, and Jamie's thrilled happiness — Jamie's happiness, if not Claudia's. Claudia smiles (that strong-but-weak, heartbreaking, polite, for-guests-only smile) and tells her daughter to *sshh* again. When Jamie gets down one of her books, Harley thinks at first she wants him to read to her, but Jamie wants to read to *him*.

They sit quietly as Jamie reads to Harley. He can hear the adults talking in the next room, speaking among themselves with a tired, day's-end relief, like outlaws holed up in a cave after a hard day's ride, having given the posse the slip.

Jack comes in and listens to the end of Jamie's story and strokes the top of her head. "My Uncle Jack," Jamie explains, pointing a thumb to yet another of her friends. Jack smiles and says to Harley, "Do you do much hunting up in Canada?"

"A little," Harley says, glancing worriedly at Jamie,

not wanting to upset her. He's still not sure of his footing in this new land, not sure if he's among brutes or effetes, or in some transition place where the two overlap and coexist. Jack grins and says, "I started bowhunting last year."

Jack had previously been almost silent, speaking only when spoken to, but now he's off and running. He begins to talk so fervently about deer hunting that everyone in the next room begins to listen and drift toward Jamie's room. Jack doesn't notice, and he keeps on, about how he got eight deer last season, how he was out in the woods every day, about camouflage, about scent.

It's as if Jack is rising from a dream or a great depth when he looks up and sees that everyone's gathered around him and is listening, and smiling.

"What," he says, stopping his story. "What's the big deal? What?"

"You," says Lois, laughing. "Doing all that *talking*."

Jack shrugs and says to Harley, "Don't listen to them. I talk plenty."

"I thought this was a la-de-da school," Harley says. "You guys are talking about hunting and fishing like you're the last of the Mohicans. This is not what I expected," he says, and Jamie giggles for no reason, and the women smile.

Willis looks smug. "Ah, it's just the three of us," he says, waving his hand toward the front door, toward the night. "The rest are all fairies. We're all we've got," he says, and Nick and Jack look down and smile, both pleased and embarrassed by the statement.

Coffee is made, and everyone goes back and sits by the big window, watching the stars and the lake, watching the moon shine, broken on the tossing waves.

"A sub went down there yesterday," Claudia says to

Harley, "the day before you got here. They just pulled the bodies out today."

"A sub?" says Harley.

"Submarine," says Shellie, nodding. "These two guys from Traverse City, engineers, built one in their garage and took it out on the lake, took it down to, what" — she looks over at Nick, who's staring at a cigarette he's just lit but isn't smoking — "a hundred feet? And the engine broke down there, and they couldn't get out, and then water started leaking in and filled the sub. They couldn't get out."

Lois shudders, and Claudia gets up, lights a cigarette, and walks over to the stereo, changes CDs.

"There's a picture of it in the paper," says Shellie. "It was a big thing, not just some little old thing. It was a real submarine."

Nick leans forward and crushes his cigarette in an ashtray. He lights another one, takes a puff, his first of the evening. He seems to be coming to life, to be stirring. "So you just live up in the woods, is that right?" he asks Harley. "Up in Canada, with nothing to do but hike and fish?"

"That's right," Harley says. He turns to the women to explain. "They gave me a bunch of money when I hurt my knees and couldn't play anymore. I'm poor now, but I get by." The women look part stricken, part fearful, but also, in that dreamlike way, perhaps . . . fascinated? wishful?

Nick crushes his cigarette after the second puff and lights a new one. Willis is looking out at the lake.

"I'd like to do that," Nick says dreamily. "Move into the woods, just read and write poetry all day." He studies his cigarette, starts to smoke it, then puts this one out, too. Shellie casts him a warning glance of some kind, a frown that in no way matches her lovely china-doll face (she's studying griffins at the nearby university; she's one of only three or four people in the country studying the stone monsters), and it's a look that neither Harley nor anyone else can understand.

"I've never been west of Louisville, Kentucky," Willis says, apropos of nothing. Harley watches as Claudia lowers her eyes.

"I've never been west of Cincinnati," says Jack, still beaming as if half tight, though there's been no drinking; he's just cheery. "I'd like to go someday, though."

"You guys'll have to come visit," says Harley. Nick lights yet another cigarette, and Willis fiddles with the volume on the stereo, lowers it a bit. Implicit in the still air are money worries, babysitters, master's theses to be finished, jobs, Little League soccer.

"At night the salmon move," Nick says, quoting a poem. Jack smiles, as does Willis, looking at Nick with an undisguised love. Harley helps Lois and Claudia clean the dishes while Shellie picks up the newspaper to look at the pictures of the salvaged submarine again.

·

The men pull their waders on over their jeans, right there in the living room, and everyone says their good-byes, does their hugging.

"Bring home a big one," Claudia says to the Wolverine. No one's supposed to eat any of the fish from the Great Lakes, they've got lead and zinc and shit in them, but the men do it anyway. The women aren't frightened either, figuring it's no worse than what they're being sold in the stores.

Jamie twists Harley's hand, trying to hold him, to keep him from leaving.

The men go out to Jack's station wagon — walking like monsters in their big waders — climb in awkwardly, and drive away. Harley notices that Nick has fallen into a funk, a trance almost, since he put the waders on, and for a minute Harley did not think that Nick was going to let go of Shellie's hand. They held each other and kissed lightly, repeatedly, as if Nick might not be coming back. It occurred to Harley that that thought had always to be in the back of Shellie's mind, that one day Nick might try to do it again. He thought about the petite, lively Shellie studying griffins in the library all day — gargoyles and demons — and felt childish, almost undeveloped. How simple his life in the woods was. He had it so easy! All he had to do was chase after Shaw and catch her each time she ran off; that was all.

But out here in the real world, there are crazy people — people playing for high stakes, men driven to launch strange inadequate submarines into lakes and pilot them straight to the bottom, drowning in graves of water . . . for no reason, and for every reason . . .

Jack drives with the high beams on, to watch for deer. The back of the station wagon is overflowing with gear: ice chests, landing nets, poles, tackle boxes, flashlights. Nick sits up front next to Jack, and Willis sits behind Nick and massages his shoulders, works the kinks in Nick's neck, the way he might rub a woman's shoulders. Harley thinks about Claudia, left behind with Jamie, and of how Claudia must have to put on some sort of sham, a semblance of happiness for their child's sake, whenever the long Michigan winter sadness comes on.

It's a long drive to the river. Clouds scud quickly past the full moon. There's a strong south wind, though it's still cold outside, almost cold enough to snow. It's like no country Harley's ever been in before — a cold *south* wind? he finds himself thinking — and Jack puts in an old hippie tape, one he's recorded himself, with Tom Rush, Tim Buckley, and Tim Hardin. Nick lights a cigarette, begins to smoke it, and looks out the window, but lowers his head again.

"Whatever happened to those guys?" Jack asks, glancing in the rear-view mirror, trying to fill the station wagon with his light, his airiness — his strength, thinks Harley. "Didn't they die? Didn't something get them?"

Willis nods. "Drugs. No, alcohol." He pauses, trying to remember. "No, a heart attack. It was one or the other. Buckley OD'd and Hardin had a heart attack, or maybe it was the other way around."

"What about Rush?" Jack asks. "That still leaves Rush."

Willis shrugs, rubbing Nick's neck again: leaning forward and kneading the thin muscles the way he would a dog's. Harley has the feeling that Nick keeps starting to say something — that he's on the verge, every time he takes a puff of his cigarette — but so far he hasn't uttered a word. The car smells like men, Harley thinks, and after living so long with only Shaw, in their cabin, with no one else around, it feels good.

For a second, as if opening his eyes under water for the briefest of instants before shutting them again, Harley thinks he sees, feels, even *understands* why Shaw runs, or rather, what she feels when she runs, though he cannot put a name on it. He pauses, tries to hold the feeling, the blurry sight of what it's like, but then he loses it, loses it like a dream, that quickly.

"I drove fifteen hours to hear him play one set — one set — at a folk festival in Provincetown, my freshman year," Jack says. "It was worth it. But I haven't heard about him in a long time."

Nick's cigarette glows in the front seat, and he starts to say something once more, then takes another puff and leans forward, tapping the ashes into the ashtray.

"He's alive," Harley says, though he has no idea who Tom Rush is. "I went out on a lake with him in a canoe this summer, up in New Hampshire. Me and my girlfriend, and he and his girlfriend. It was real nice. We had a real good time." Harley feels as if he's under water again, his eyes open, swimming hard, looking for Shaw.

"Did he play?" Jack asks, fascinated. "Did he play his guitar?"

"He played and sang," Harley says. "Loons were crying all around us, diving and bobbing all around the boat, and it was real quiet, right at dusk. The acoustics were perfect. He sat out on the bow — we barely all fit — and he played and sang for over an hour."

Jack's watching Harley in the rear-view mirror. "Was he still good?" he asks.

"Oh, he was wonderful," Harley says. "It was as lovely an evening as you can imagine. His girlfriend is a friend of my girlfriend's. We went swimming after we came back in to shore, and then Tom fixed pork loins with some kind of wild raspberry sauce poured over them. He lives in this big castle kind of place with lots of flowers out in the garden, but does his own cooking." Harley's lying like mad, trying to bring Shaw back in to him, and trying to keep Nick from leaping off any bridges, too.

"In the morning we had strawberry waffles. Joni Mitchell called and was coming by later that afternoon, but we had to go, we had to be somewhere. He gave us a bunch of his albums and a jug of maple syrup and wild honey that he'd made."

Harley says, "He's still alive, he's in good shape."

They ride the rest of the way to the Platte in silence, listening to the tape. It's like they're all five friends now, the four men and Tom Rush, admitted into their circle. Old Tom, old pork-loin-cooking Tom, one of the guys — Tom Rush, who survived: and they listen to the guitar, listen to the tape, and drive through the night, through the dark trees.

Jack reaches over and squeezes Nick's thigh. "Tonight's the night, bucko," he says. "Tonight your luck's going to change. Tonight you're going to catch your first steelhead."

Nick groans, and Willis laughs. "He's been fishing hard all year," he explains, "but he hasn't caught one yet." Nick groans again, and Harley likes, even loves, the fact that there are no secrets among the three friends. They don't treat Nick like a leper or anything just because he hasn't caught a single steelhead, hasn't even *hooked* one, while they, Jack and Willis, the Wolverine, have been catching them pretty regularly all season long. Sometimes two or three in a single night, and always big ones, monsters: adults, spawners, sneaking up the river to lay eggs and spray sperm, then die. Big bulls and sows, blunt-nosed, glimmering, marching up the river at night.

Nick groans again and finally says what it is he's been trying to say all along, taking one last puff of his cigarette before crumpling it in the ashtray.

"I should kill myself," he says, looking out the window at nothing. He laughs a mean, lost laugh. Harley's heard the phrase uttered hundreds of times — he's even said it himself a few times — but he's never heard it said the way Nick says it.

They stop at the first bridge, and like boys they get out and sneak along the railing until they're over the center of the river with their flashlights. They peer over the edge, shine their lights down into the fast-moving, shallow water to see if the steelhead are running, if they're moving upriver yet. It's not quite midnight.

"I see one," the Wolverine says, pointing. "There!" They all see it then, a dark shadow like a shark — a big shadow nearly two feet long — steadying itself, moving slowly against the current.

They all study the fish for a long time, the flashlight's beam faltering as the battery weakens; then, with a quick flip of its tail, the fish's shadow shoots upstream, and the shallow river is empty again. The men turn and run to the other side of the bridge, the upstream side, but the fish is gone and there are no others, not at this point, anyway.

"They haven't really started yet," Jack says. "I'll bet they're still down at the mouth of the river. We can still get into them down there." They hurry like commandos back to the car, get in, and drive again.

When they arrive at a hot spot, a honey hole — just upstream of where the river enters the lake — there are smelt fishermen, cretins and barbarians, wading at the river's mouth with nets and lanterns, inadvertently blocking the salmon from entering the river. The smelt netters try to catch the more numerous, dumber fish: a sport for old men and mental patients, Jack tells Harley.

Willis wades into the water and talks to the smelt netters for a while, and then their lanterns go off. The netters — there are three of them — come out of the river, get in their car, and drive away.

"What did you tell them?" Jack asks.

"The truth," Willis says. "That we had a manic-depressive with us, that he wanted to try and catch a steelhead, that it might be the last year of his life, and that they were blocking the steelhead's return to the river with their stupid lanterns and yo-yo nets."

Nick smiles, a bit sadly, and nods.

"And they *left?*" Jack asks, amazed.

The Wolverine shrugs. "Well, I told them some other things, too."

Harley laughs, and feels like a savage.

There's a long walk through the woods to the sharp bend in the river where the men like to fish. They're headed for a steep bluff on the outside of the bend, and on the inside there's a shoal and ankle-deep shallows. Between the bluff and the shoal is a deep channel that runs down the middle of the river. It may be thirty feet deep, says Willis, but it may be bottomless, too. That's where the salmon are, moving up and down it, to and from the lake, and the way to catch them is to cast fluorescent yellow and orange marshmallow-looking flies (resembling salmon eggs) into that channel and let them free-drift, hopefully into a salmon's jaws.

"Don't get too near the channel," Willis warns Harley, handing him a fly rod. "It's shallow, no more than waist-deep all the way out into the current, but then once you step off the shelf and into the channel, you'll go straight down, especially in those waders you've got on. Straight to the bottom. We had to pull old Nick out of here twice last year."

The men are standing in the trees on the far side of the river, beside an abandoned hunting cabin, where the river straightens and is only chest-deep in the middle. They will cross there to get over to the shallows on the other side, in order to cast back into the deep channel.

"Follow our footsteps exactly," Jack says, easing into the river. The stars are bright all around them. It's so lonely that it's exciting. Harley feels as if something big could happen at any second.

"Don't get out of our footsteps," Willis says as he and Nick enter the river. "We know where to go."

Harley can't swim, but with the waders on, it wouldn't matter if he could. He's at the river's mercy, and it's flowing from left to right as he steps into the water behind them. He feels like a sea creature returning to the ocean, some evolutionary throwback trying to reverse history. The water's cold even through the rubber waders, ice cold, and the current's strong — stronger than he is, Harley can tell in an instant.

The men hold their fly rods over the top of their heads and cross the mystery spot that only they know about, with the water rising quickly above their knees, above their waists, and then almost up to their chests. They take several steps like that, too many, so that surely they are marching toward their doom. The sound of the river is loud in Harley's ears, the river just a foot or so below his chin and trying to sweep him away. But then, like a blessing, they're climbing out again. Once they're on the other side it all seems silly, like there was never any danger, and they're ready to fish. They're rigging up their lines, tying on the blaze-yellow artificial flies.

Walking through the woods, on his way down to the river, following Nick and the others — ducking branches and trying to avoid the briars — had been like chasing Shaw through the woods at home, Harley thought — exactly. And he had the feeling, as the men walked in silence ahead of him, that each of them knew, somehow intuitively, what Harley was going through, the tremble and terror of Shaw's packing, one box at a time, leaving. And Harley was sure too that each of the men ahead of him knew, as if they could read his mind, how he chased Shaw through the woods once a month, through the snowdrifts, leaping fallen logs, floundering, and then tackling her and carrying her back.

He had the feeling that not only was his secret being read, but that those men had gone through the very same thing — had chased their wives before, lost them, caught them, let them go, chased them, found them — and that the reason no one was saying anything as they walked, with the stars scattered bright around them, was that they were all the same. There was no need to speak.

•

It's a slow night. They stand in the waist-deep water in the dark, at the edge of the trough. It's gurgling and splashing, lifting cool air to their faces and pressing against their legs, as if trying to draw them in. They cast their flies back and forth into the trough's heart, into the crease, saying nothing, just the four of them, waiting and staring at the empty cabin on the other side of the river, the bluff side. Their flies hang for a second on the back-cast above their heads, the tiny yellow flies mixed in with the stars before being launched forward, floating down to the river and then drifting, riding the center's mad rush, waiting to be taken by the cruising steelhead. The men on the other end of the thin line stare into near dark-ness at the fast black water, waiting for that shoulder-jolt sock, the yank like an electrocution that tells them that lure and fish and man have connected. There are hundreds of salmon, perhaps, cruising up river, up the trough in the darkness, but no way to tell, there's only hope, and the longer the four men go without a bite, the more it feels like the salmon aren't coming, like it's a bad night, or maybe there aren't any salmon left any-more, perhaps they're all gone, or uncatchable.

It's an hour before one bites. "Fish!" cries Jack, lifting his rod into a bow, a flexing, slender half circle. Harley's surprised to see that they're so technical about it, crying "Fish!" rather than the more spontaneous, boyish "Got one!" Everyone else reels in and backs up into the shallows to keep from tangling lines as the big steelhead leaps, its belly silver in the moonlight. Harley leans forward, imagines he can see the fish's bulging eyes, the gasp of its mouth, the fight of a lifetime, with everything at stake, too much at stake. Willis, Harley, and Nick stand back by the sandbar, poles in hand, and watch as Jack, not grinning for once, passes through wooded shafts of moonlight, the strips of light working across his arms, his face, the river. Jack's following the big fish downriver, stumbling sometimes; the fish is running for the lake, using the strong current to help it. Jack splashes through the shallows, trying to keep up and give the fish some semblance of a fight, trying to tire it out so he can reel it in without snapping the thin piano-wire line, the line that the poets in Jack's and Willis's and Nick's art school refer to, in olden poems, as "gossamer."

Nine times out of ten, the big fish simply snaps the leader, and is gone (the tiny hook rusts away and falls out of the fish's mouth after a day or two, Willis tells Harley, leaving no one injured, only wiser). But this time Jack is able to land the steelhead, to wear it down and drag it up on the sandbar.

It's the most beautiful thing Harley's ever seen come out of the water — fluorescent red, emerald, stony black, chocolate brown, and moon silver. It's nearly dead from the fight. Willis turns the flashlight off, and Jack unhooks the tiny fly from beside the fish's jaw and goes off into the brush to find a stick. He comes back and thwacks it twice, three times, solidly on the head. The big fish — twelve pounds, maybe thirteen, Jack says, breathing heavily — dies then. The spirit of the fish flies up to the stars, and the glittering corpse remains on the sandbar. Nick stares blankly at the fish, and then lights a cigarette. The other men wade back into the river.

They fish for a long time afterward, with no action — none. Just the motion: casting back and forth, back and forth, but believing, now. Harley glances at his watch when the moon steps from behind some clouds — two A.M. — and looks back at the sandbar, where Nick's still standing, just a silhouette in the shadows. Nick's staring off in some nondirection, thinking about something far away, and simply not moving: almost perfectly motionless, Harley thinks, casting back and forth. Like a statue.

Raccoons prowl along the sandbar, trilling to one another as if plotting how to get closer to the fish, paws groping delicately in the cold shallows, feeling for mussels. Their eyes are bright as they pass through those striped patches of moonlight, and they fix their stares on the men standing in the river, as if jealous of them, before resuming their probing.

Eventually the raccoons are brave enough to cluster around Nick — Jack watches, fascinated — but still they don't touch the fish, though they look at it and chirr even more.

Nick stands on the sandbar among the raccoons, smoking. All Jack and Harley can see is his silhouette and the end of his glowing cigarette.

Harley and Jack go back to fishing. An hour passes, maybe more, and the raccoons leave. Nick does, too. He wades downstream of the cabin, walking without a flashlight, and disappears into the woods, headed back to the car. The smell of his cigarette hangs over the river for a while, and then there's nothing, just the cold emptiness of April waiting to open up into May. And the fish, perhaps, snaking their way, hidden, upstream — ignoring the bright lures, trying to make it past the devil-tempter men.

"Is Nick okay?" Willis asks Jack. "Do you think we ought to go check on him?"

Jack shakes his head grimly. There's little doubt that he's replaying the night's fight — the big belly of the steelhead leaping, the mad pull down the river. "He's just down, is all," Jack says, feeling the drift of his line, staring out at the river's blackness. "There's nothing we can do."

Harley hears Jack grunt when the next steelhead hits, and feels, twenty yards downstream, Jack's near terror, and then pleasure, and then, quickly, Jack's determination as Jack lifts the rod, arches it, sets the hook, and begins the shuffling dance, headed Harley's way, down the river, hooked onto another fish.

"Fish," Jack mutters, almost under his breath. The fish, rising like a rocket, surges. It twists, shakes, rolls, and crashes back into the river, leaps again, but still it's hooked. Jack has it on his line — it's still Jack's fish, Jack *owns* this piece of wildness, and it's a fight, nothing but a fight, and there will be no compromise, the fish is too large. It will be landed and clubbed and taken home and eaten (the way it has eaten other fish all its life) — or it will escape.

"Here," Jack says, sidestepping past Harley, starting downstream after the runaway fish. Line is stripping out with a high, fast clicking sound, a *zing*, the fish taking Jack's line, and his reel and rod, and even Jack, all the way back to the lake, even perhaps to the sea. "Here," Jack says, holding the bowing rod out to Harley. "Take it."

Harley freezes. He's petrified.

"It's your fish," Harley says, and shakes his head. "No. You go ahead."

"Hurry," Jack insists. "Take it."

Harley steps up and takes the bouncing, vibrating rod from Jack's strong hands. Harley has long forgotten that these men are poets; it could be a century ago that he had been told that fact. What it feels like, to Harley, is that he has hooked into a linebacker. He might as well be standing on a football field, having cast his fly toward the jersey of an all-American, and that all-American is running down the field, running toward Canada, surfing down the center of the river, under water, running. Harley digs in and tries to hold the big fish, but it's no good, the fish is too strong, too fast. The line is being stripped off the reel as fast as it can go, and Harley, like Jack before him, begins to run along through the shallows, following the huge fish's flight: raising the rod every now and then, trying to provide some resistance, trying to slow the fish down, but all the fish feels is fear, and Harley stumbles along behind it, his line almost gone, and then, at the end of the sandbar, it is gone.

Harley stops, digs in, raises the rod, and begins trying to reel the fish in. He can barely turn the crank, and he wonders, with a shock, if Jack's stronger than he is — Jack had been able to land *his* fish — and the fish leaps once, and Harley pulls harder, trying to reel it in, and then there's a soft, earthy pull, and a looseness, like a bad tooth coming out, an emptiness that the tongue quickly runs itself over. In the dark like that, Harley hasn't really seen anything, just the fish's huge silver form leaping once, right before it broke the leader. It's a feeling that will give him nightmares for months afterward. And he stands there with the loose line, the empty

rod, and swears, swears in his heart, that he can feel the
fish (a part of himself now) still running, out to the lake
already — out to the lake.

.

On the way home, they stop off at the upstream
bridge again. Nick stays in the car, but the other three
shine their lights down on the river, and this time they
see them — ten, twelve, maybe more — long, dark steelhead nosing their way up the river like submarines, moving from rock to rock, surging and then faltering — dark
shadows against the river's stony bottom.

"They're here," Willis whispers, shutting off his flashlight and looking over at Jack, who's shut his light off
too, and is crouched, looking over the edge, still watching the dark, fishy shadows in the moonlight, breathing
raggedly. Like a big cat, thinks Harley, like a tiger.

"Should we tell him?" Willis asks. He wants fish, but
he also knows he should get his friend home, that Nick
has had enough fishing. That maybe Shellie, in bed, with
her smallness and her warmth, can gather him in and
hold him until the season passes — her textbooks on
griffins, on monstrosities, closed on her desk. Jack looks
crazy, wild-haired in the moonlight, glancing from Willis
to the river and back. All those fish below, bodies and
bodies of fish, just waiting.

"We've got to go," Willis says. He even laughs a low
laugh, almost a mean sound, and yet with some humor
in it, some belief in the future. "We've got to get him
home. We've been gone too long already."

"Yes," says Jack, easing up, looking at the river one
more time. "Yes," he says again, sighing. Harley has the
feeling Jack is thinking now of hunting season, four
months distant. They walk back to the car.

"Well?" says Nick in a dull voice, his head down between his legs. "Well?"

No one says anything, and they ride home in wet waders, returning slowly to earth. The big fish in the back is wrapped in newspaper, like a flower, and smells fishy, but fresh, like the river.

They stop for gas at a twenty-four-hour convenience store, brightly lit, more or less in the middle of nowhere. There's just one woman working the cash register — a young girl, actually, no older than the high school students Jack, Nick, and Willis teach.

The four men stand around the car in their waders and heavy sweaters as Nick, trying to resurface, to revive, fills the car with gas. They are eager to go in and talk to the young girl, who looks so lonely, and who's watching them with a hard, old-yet-young interest — but they can't abandon Nick.

A few moths bounce against the bright yellow lights over their heads. The convenience store's parking lot, in all its middle-of-the-blackness brilliance, could be a landing spot for flying saucers, Harley thinks.

Nick shuts the pump off and the four men, in squishing boots, walk in, blinking like owls, and smile at the girl, who grins back. They begin buying their junk food: greasy doughnuts and potato chips. Nick buys some more cigarettes, and they all buy beer nuts and acid coffee. They ask the girl how her classes are going. She's not in school, it turns out; she's got a daughter a year old. The girl, who isn't wearing a name tag, won't tell them her name, but asks if they caught anything.

"Nope," says Jack, grinning.

It's just a pleasure to be in her company. Jack buys a lottery ticket, rubs off the numbers, and wins two dollars. The girl smiles. Jack trades in the winning ticket for two more and hands one to Harley and one to Nick, but neither of them wins anything.

"I'll go home with y'all," the girl says. The whole world seems empty, lonely. The men laugh and look down, considering it, and then glance at one another. The girl doesn't understand that there's no chance of this happening, and for a moment she gets her hopes up: it's got to be like having a fish on the line.

"We're married," Jack says after a long pause, though that's not it at all. What it is, is that it's late, everyone's tired and needs a shower and sleep. But Jack says this with a wonderful sly grin, as if to show that he, and all of them, are considering it. And so the girl smiles, not at all daunted, and says, "Here, take these," and hands them a big box of doughnuts.

"Why, thank you," says Jack, tipping his baseball cap. The girl beams, delighted with her four new boyfriends. As they're leaving, Nick stops and takes off his wrist-watch — it's silver, heavy, expensive — and gives it to her.

They drive on into the night, eating stale doughnuts, drinking bad coffee.

"She didn't mean all of us," Willis says with his mouth full. "She meant any of us. I'll bet she meant you, Nick." Willis reaches up in the front seat and offers him a doughnut, and Nick shakes his head.

"Messy," says Jack, grinning, looking back. "Messy, messy." He plugs in the Tom Rush tape, and they all think about Harley's lie, about being on the lake with Rush, perfect acoustics, close enough to touch him.

"Season's over," Jack says when they reach Nick's house and let him out. They all shake hands, even though they'll see him only a few hours later, at school.

"Next year," Willis says to Nick.

Nick walks around to the back of the car, takes his rod out, and hands it to Willis. "I want you to have this," he says.

Jack and Willis look at each other.

"Just take it, Wolverine," Nick says, pressing it into Willis's hands. Nick laughs an odd, false laugh, the kind that might dissolve into weeping if Willis doesn't take the rod.

"Thank you," Willis says, and puts the rod back in the car. He feels as if he's aided in whatever's coming. Later, playing the scene back, he wishes he'd done it another way — thought of the right thing to say in order to refuse the rod.

Nick also tries to give Jack his new sleeveless down vest. It had given them the illusion that Nick had some bulk, but Jack, who even without the puffy vest is larger than Nick, refuses it sternly. Jack tells him *no* so forcefully that it hurts Nick's feelings. Nick smiles a strange, sad smile, as if Jack's missing his chance to get in on the ground floor of some unbelievable deal. Nick nods goodbye to Jack, who's still bristling, and shakes Willis's hand, then walks slowly, carrying his vest over his arm like a blanket, through the trees to his dark cottage.

The men watch him go. Each of them imagines Shellie sleeping in the warm, dry house. Harley imagines her in a flannel nightgown; Willis imagines her in sweat pants and a T-shirt; and Jack imagines her in a robe, sitting on the edge of the bed, rubbing her eyes, having heard the car drive up, wondering if Nick's all right — trying to psych herself up into believing that he is — and maybe hoping that he caught a fish. She hears him come in and knows instantly that he did not.

The three men sit in the car for a second and watch

Nick's house, but when no lights come on, they back up and drive away.

·

It's a bright, windy morning when Willis comes by Harley's cottage to pick him up, about ten minutes before class. Harley's lying on his stomach, snoring, with the windows open. The curtains are blowing wildly. He's dreaming of Shaw's scarves, of their amazing colors, and of the way, before she sends them off to a gallery or museum, she'll have them tacked up over the whole side of the barn as she sits below them in a lawn chair, at a slight distance, and evaluates them, trying to decide which ones to send — all of them fluttering and snapping in the Canadian air. In his dream, he sees for the first time that there are worse things than being deserted, left behind. He feels a mild peace.

Willis sits down on the edge of the bed. He shakes Harley's shoulder lightly, and then roughly.

"Wake up, Heine Man," he says. "Wake up."

·

They walk to class together. Harley's still wearing what he had on the night before, though he's changed into sneakers and has a night's beard. But he looks strangely fresh after having washed his face and combed his hair. The cold wind is invigorating. The wind's stiff, turned around from the north, coming off the lake. Harley, who still hasn't given the first speck of thought to what it is he is going to talk about, feels like a tumbling leaf in the fall.

He remembers walking back with the Wolverine from college football practice, in weather so cold that their sweaty hair froze solid. He remembers the clacking sound their hair made as they walked. He remembers being so fucking strong.

Eleven hours, Harley thinks — thirteen, counting the time change — before he sees Shaw, or rather, before he sees their cabin and finds out whether she has finished packing and left. Thirteen more hours. Harley tries to think of the class, and of what he might have to offer, but he can't. Then he tries to think of Shaw again, but as he and Willis walk side by side, hands in their pockets, saying nothing, what Harley realizes they are both thinking about is Nick, and his giveaway program of the night before.

It's like a fish running for the sea, Harley thinks, trying to stop a thing like that, when someone's got a case of it as bad as Nick does.

"Did you remember to get that fish out of the back?" Harley asks.

"Yes," says Willis. He looks up, grinning, remembering Jack fighting the fish. Remembers standing in the river himself, in the night, as if he were another creature, as if it were another life. "Sorry you won't be here to eat it," he says.

"Ah," says Harley, coming to life and looking out at the lake, swinging a hand at the head of a bare thistle along the trail they're walking down. "It was fun just to see it caught."

•

The students are already there. Dressed in black, all hip and bright-eyed, many of them still have wet clinging hair from their showers. He sees what he knows must be poets, composers, singers, musicians: flutists, cellists, pianists, bassists. Harley thinks of Shaw: a whole school of little Shaws — or a whole classroom, anyway.

He stands at the front of the class. The Wolverine has abandoned him, deposited him in the room like a brown bear dumping a salmon onto the bank for her cubs to feed on. Willis sits at the back of the class with his hands clasped behind his head, red-eyed, smiling.

Nick comes by and peers through the doorway. Spying Harley up there alone, he nods good morning to him and tosses a brown paper bag across the room. Embarrassed, Harley catches it, but does not open it. Nick waves goodbye and disappears.

Out on the grassy quad, the carillon bells begin to ring. Harley clears his throat, shrugs, and looks around the room. He has no idea what to say. It's like the worst of nightmares. Harley glances from student to student and is terrified to see the suspicion beginning to light in their young eyes, their dark artists' eyes.

Then Willis walks up to the front, opening windows as he goes. Fresh, cold air swirls into the classroom. The students turn to watch him as he clears some empty desks out of the way, so there's more space around Harley — and now, even more, it looks as if the class has Harley trapped.

"This man is strong, stronger than any of us will ever be," Willis says, pointing to Harley as if he's diagramming a poem — talking about its structure, perhaps. "He's got talent, too, but mostly he's just strong. I thought we'd show you what this man used to do for a living. He was so good at it that in two years of doing this, he made enough money — not that money is any kind of measurement — to last him, if he's frugal, the rest of his life."

"What does he do now?" one of the students asks, a tall, thin, pale boy, an inner-city-looking kid with long black hair and a blue-jean jacket. Harley wants to take this boy under his wing, carry him to Canada and teach him to drive fence posts, rather than let him write poems or play the trumpet, or whatever pretty thing it is that he does.

"He walks in the woods," Willis says before Harley can answer. He indicates Harley with his pointer as if, still, Harley were only a poem. "He makes love to his girlfriend. He gets up early in the morning and goes to bed early. He lives in the woods." Willis grows more animated, tapping the pointer in the palm of his hand. "He doesn't have a family, doesn't have any responsibilities, and he doesn't even have a job." Willis taps Harley with the pointer.

Willis turns and stares out the window. *"He just walks in the woods,"* he says again, and turns back to the class. "If Harley doesn't mind, and if his knees aren't bothering him, I thought we'd demonstrate what we used to do — how he used to block people out of the way, to protect me while I ran all over the field, skittering around more or less like a chicken with his head cut off." The class laughs, and they lean forward in their seats and look at Willis, and then at Harley, and then back at Willis, their teacher.

Willis glances over at Harley, and Harley shrugs and nods.

"I'll be the defender," Willis says, setting aside the pointer in a corner. "I used to run with Harley, but today I'll pretend like I'm on the other side and am trying to get past him — trying to get past him to get to *me*. Pretend there's a running back behind him. That's what I used to be. That's where I used to be.

"Harley's going to block me and keep me from getting behind him. He's going to keep me from getting back there and tackling that runner."

Willis crouches down. He's wearing slick-bottomed street shoes, and Harley realizes this wasn't premeditated. Harley crouches, remembering everything: every practice under the hot fall blue skies, every day with his friend Willis, every day walking back to the dorm after practice. Then he remembers the pros, the traveling, the namelessness of it, the roaring maw of the stadium crowds, and the way it wasn't so much fun anymore — and what it feels like to Harley is that Nick's back there, and that Harley's trying to protect Nick, and even Willis's sad winter-sick wife, Claudia, and their hopeful little girl, Jamie — everyone who ever mattered a damn is slipping in behind Harley, getting back there behind him and hiding, for protection, everyone but Shaw, who doesn't need Harley anymore, who's gone.

And for the next half hour or so, as the class watches, fascinated, the two men struggle and clash like dinosaurs: feinting, shuffling back and forth, locked in combat, crashing into one another. Harley knocks the Wolverine to the ground repeatedly, and each time, tenaciously, nearly growling, the Wolverine comes back harder and faster, trying to slip past Harley, trying to get behind him, but he can't, he doesn't, Harley's still got it, and it's why they paid him so much.

Finally both men can't go on any longer, and they stand, half bent over, gasping, sweat streaming down their foreheads, down their chests. Their shirts stick to them, damp across the backs, across their tight chests, and they just stare at each other, panting, not yet friends again.

The class begins to applaud, which snaps Harley and Willis out of the gasping and staring they were locked into. Willis rises from his crouch first and picks up the pointer, and then Harley straightens up.

"Talk," Willis says, tapping Harley with the pointer. "Talk your heart out."

"I never learned to let anything go past me," Harley says, gasping as if for his life. "I have to learn to let things go past." He shrugs. "I have to go against my instinct. I still have to learn that." He's breathing like a locomotive and still sweating wildly, as if being tortured. "It takes me years to learn things," he says.

The students listen intently to his confession.

"I learn with my body quickly," Harley says, "but I learn with my mind slow. It's almost impossible," he says, "to let something go. I was the best there was at not letting anything get past. I was too damn fucking good. It turned me into a fucking *crustacean*."

Willis nods proudly, as if Harley has found out something that Willis has known all his life, and yet also as if Harley has reminded Willis of a forgotten secret, a great mysterious one.

"Show and tell," Willis says to the class, still breathing hard. "Next we'll touch this man, to see what it's like to be as strong as he is." Willis walks over and begins unbuttoning Harley's shirt, and helps him out of it. Harley's breathing hard, too tired to protest, and he's too lost, as well, in the memories — the hitting, the blocking, the defending.

The cool air sweeping in through the windows feels wonderful. Willis hands Harley the shirt, and he wads it up and towels off with it, then sits down.

"Come on," Willis says, motioning to the class, pointing to a black girl first, and then to the pale boy behind her, and then to the girl behind him, a tall, shy girl with large glasses and lots of red hair, a poet. "Come *on*," Willis urges, gesturing them up with the pointer. "Don't be shy. Come feel him."

One by one, starting with the black girl — who's wearing a white blouse, navy skirt, and navy sweater — the other students fall in line behind her. They walk past Harley and touch the parts of him (as he sits there heaving, panting, shoulders rising and falling, heart racing) that they want to touch.

The black girl cups her hands over the smooth round melons of Harley's chest, then strokes his bull neck with her fingers lightly, and passes on, out the door. The pale boy touches one of Harley's blood-filled arms, carefully at first, but then taps it — again, as if it's a melon, a ripe fruit — and then squeezes it with both of his hands, grins. "A *crustacean,* man," he says, and then moves on.

The tall girl with the red hair and big glasses dips down and feels Harley's face, his jaw, and then runs her hand down the flatness of his bare stomach. Now, growing more confident, more familiar, she pats it twice, the way she might pat a puppy's stomach.

The whole class moves past him, a procession, and he's still breathing hard. He closes his eyes and remembers the days in the stadium, all the days leading up to this one — and all the days that lie ahead of him, with or without Shaw — and finally feels that he has earned his money today.

He sits there with his eyes closed after the last student has left the room. It is just Harley and Willis again, the two of them sitting alone in the classroom, the windows open, and both of them purged, so that it could be twenty years ago again and both of them just hanging out in a classroom in Ohio, after chemistry lecture and before spring practice. A single fly buzzes inside, high against the warm glass of the open window. Spring is coming hard to northern Michigan. Harley glances at his watch; he's still got an hour or so before his plane leaves, so they sit there a while, heads leaned back like reptiles, resting, just breathing.

Then Willis asks, "What's in the bag?"

Harley leans forward slowly looks inside it, and smiles, shakes his head.

"A shirt," he says. "A fancy button-down long-sleeve dress shirt."

"Put it on," Willis says lazily.

Harley stands up and tries it on. It's too short in the sleeves, it's tight under the arms and especially across the chest — the fabric stretched and the buttons straining to pop — but it's a crisp, clean white shirt, and it will do well for the flight back home, where Shaw may or may not be waiting. Harley looks down at the new shirt, which smells like Nick — which makes him feel, in that secret way that another's clothing can do, that he *is* Nick, only without Nick's sadness — and he smiles. Willis reaches in his pocket and takes out the check — the fifteen hundred dollars — and hands it to Harley.

•

"He's been trying to give his stuff away for two weeks now," Willis says when they get to the airport.

Harley shakes his head, looks down at his feet. "Do you think he'll do it?" he asks.

The Wolverine becomes very quiet, very somber. He shrugs, looks up at his friend. "I don't know," he says. "It's not something I, or anyone, has any control over. Shit," Willis says, looking helpless for the first time that Harley can remember, "it's a force of nature. Either he will or he won't. I've got no control over it."

Harley nods distractedly and tugs once more on the sleeves, which are trying to creep up his thick forearms. He leans forward and hugs the Wolverine hard — it may be twenty years before they see each other again, he thinks. It looks for a moment as if they are wrestling. Then Harley turns and goes through the boarding gate.

.

Five years later, Harley finds himself on one of the San Juan Islands with two women. One of the women is someone whom Harley's only just begun dating; the other is married, a friend of Harley's new woman friend. Shaw's been gone forever. Harley still misses her. His arms, still huge, remind him of what a fucking crustacean he is. Though he has not talked to the Wolverine since he last saw him in Michigan, Harley sometimes watches the mail, waiting to hear how Nick is doing. And hearing nothing, he has to assume that all is well: that they're still taking care of him, holding him, taking care of each other — and that maybe Nick is better. No news is almost like good news, Harley thinks. Nothing's gotten past. He doesn't think it has, anyway.

It's May, and windy as hell on top of the hill they're looking out from. There are humped islands below them, like the backs of animals, out in the Strait of Juan de Fuca. They're in Friday Harbor. To the west and north, Victoria Island, and Canada.

It's cold. They've all got on coats. The three of them are sharing one pair of binoculars and are watching for killer whales — orcas — which some biologists think get trapped in the strait, turned around in their migrations, though others believe the whales come in among the islands for protection from Pacific storms.

Harley and his two friends aren't seeing any whales, however. Instead, they watch the huge ships that nose slowly through the Inside Passage. The water is bright blue. Just scant miles away is Vancouver Island, where many of the people speak a foreign language, Harley thinks — French.

It's all still so exotic to him, he thinks — everything. Whales, and foreign languages, and so much new country — so much new *shit*. He can't figure out what the two women want with him — why they are interested in him, when he is so simple. He feels he has no complexity whatsoever, and understands almost nothing.

He feels how firm and cold the ground is beneath his sturdy legs, his heavy boots.

"I can't make out the words on that tanker," Ginny, the married woman, says, peering through the glasses. She's in her late forties, only a year or two older than Harley, and attractive.

Willa, Harley's friend, is thirty.

"D-O-C —" Ginny begins.

The wind picks up, blurs the image in the binoculars, and Ginny hands them to Harley and rubs her eyes. "It looks like Docen-something," she says.

Harley squints at the tanker. It looks foreign, somehow, though he can't tell why, and he can't tell if it's coming or going, though he has a feeling — again, somehow — that it's going. "D-O-C-E-N-C-L-A-V-E?" he says hopefully, only half believing in himself and what he's seeing.

"It could be N-A-V-E," says Willa, who has worked on a fishing boat up in Alaska. "Navy. Could be Liberian registry, or Panamanian." Willa's light on her toes, twisting and jumping in the wind, fresh, and doesn't seem to feel the sadness that Harley and Ginny are feeling — feeling and trying not to show or even acknowledge. Willa turns her face up toward Harley, who's still squinting through the binoculars, and says, "We could call up the customs office and ask them where it's from, and where it's going."

Willa turns again, catches her hat in the wind. "I'm always doing stuff like that, wasting money on long-distance calls," she says. "Here," she says, reaching for the binoculars, "let me see." Harley hands them to her. The wind's cold.

"D-O-E-N-A-V-E," Willa spells. She can see better than Harley or Ginny. But she still doesn't know what it means — none of them do. Willa takes Harley's hand in hers and squeezes it, twists her fingers around his, then hands the binoculars to Ginny.

Ginny's still watching the ship, but not with the binoculars. She gazes at it as if she's about to go to it, as if she's got a ticket, or as if she's employed on it and has missed the port of call. She's watching it like it's *her* ship.

"Don't you ever wish you could just get on a ship like that?" she asks, and Harley feels pretty sure she's talking just to him. "Wouldn't it be great if you could just jump on a ship like that and ride, and go wherever it's going?"

She's speaking as if in a trance, and turns, with her eyes watering in the wind, to look up at Harley — half happy and half hopeful, imagining it.

"Yes," says Harley, understanding, finally.

About the Author

RICK BASS lives on a remote ranch in northern Montana. His stories have appeared in *The Paris Review, Esquire, Antæus,* and *The Quarterly* and have been anthologized in *The Best American Short Stories 1988, 1991,* and *1992; New Stories from the South; Prize Stories: The O. Henry Awards;* and *The Pushcart Prize.* In 1988 he won the PEN/Nelson Algren Award, Special Citation. He is the author of *The Watch* and *In the Loyal Mountains,* two collections of prizewinning stories, and five books about the outdoors, including *Oil Notes, Winter,* and *The Ninemile Wolves.* He is working on a nonfiction book about searching for grizzly bears in Colorado and on a novel, *Where the Sea Used to Be.*